ALSO BY SHARON GERLACH

Harper & Lyttle Series
Office Politics
The Secret Dreams of Sarah-Jane Quinn

The Devil's Mansion Series
The Wyckham House
Condemned

Blackberry House Series
Where I Belong
Simon Says

Single Titles
Burning Books

A **Running Ink Press** novella

Running Ink Press, LLC
1419 N Lee St
Spokane WA 99202

Copyright ©2011 Sharon Gerlach
ISBN: 0983291233
ISBN 13: 978-0-9832912-3-7
www.runninginkpress.com

Edited by NL Gervasio
Cover design by Sharon Gerlach
Cover image © 2004 Jan Bily

First Running Ink Press paperback printing: October 2011

Printed in the U.S.A.

ACKNOWLEDGEMENTS

While the actual writing of a book is a solitary endeavor, no book is truly ever completed alone. From research to beta-reading to editing to publication, many hands craft a story into magic your eyes can behold.

My family, who often has only my divided attention and puts up with me being tethered to technology all the time.

My awesome husband Gail, who knows a little about darn near everything or knows where to find the information I need.

My Merry Band of Beta Readers, who faithfully read every word I churn out onto paper—be it gold or pot metal: Christel, Nikki, Denise, Gini, and Julia, you are indispensable.

Editor Extraordinaire, NL Gervasio, who busts my chops on my run-on sentences and won't let me put anything really stupid into my work.

MALAKH

sharon gerlach

"The sons of God saw that the daughters of men were beautiful,"
and they married any of them they chose."

Genesis 6:2
(NIV)

Chapter One

"Lost in your thoughts and not paying attention to where you're going," drawled a voice nearby.

I jumped, belatedly looking up. I had been walking to my car on auto-pilot after leaving the deli, not paying attention to my surroundings—a recipe for disaster. But I didn't worry very much about being attacked; all I needed to receive invincible help was to call out a name. I hoped I would never have to.

He lounged against my car door, ankles crossed, negligently examining his fingernails. I wasn't fooled; I knew his eyes never left my face. And I knew what he was, although he looked human enough—the ringing quality to his voice, as though his vocal cords were made of crystal, was unique to his species. He wore his human guise with a trace of disdain he was unable to completely hide, and his handsomeness was just a shade too perfect and somehow...blurred around the edges.

"No," I said, shaking my head. "Whatever you want, I can't help you. I'm not getting involved with your kind again."

"Once involved, always involved." His eyes half-closed, he sniffed the air. "I smell him on you, Suzanne, faint but unmistakable."

"It's been three years," I snapped, crossing my arms over my chest even though such an action was futile. There was no hiding anything from them.

"You know why I'm here. Your heart mourns more than

just his love; it mourns what you know he's become. Will you hear me out?"

He stepped away from the car, and quicker than a thought pulled the lapel of my silk blouse open, exposing the upper slope of my right breast above its lacy covering. His finger pressed the jagged scar that rose from the edge of my lace bra.

"You bear his mark; you have an obligation."

"It's not him." I didn't say it with conviction, but in denial. The truth was I didn't *want* it to be him. I couldn't wrap my mind around the possibility that my former lover had turned to serial murder.

He backed away from me and held out his hands, palms up. A gesture of subservience. An invitation to join forces. "Ten minutes of your time, that's all I ask."

"Who sent you?"

"I take orders from none but the highest."

I stared down at his hands, at their lineless palms like smooth, sun-blushed marble. My mind in turmoil, I took a step away from him. No, I couldn't possibly consider it. Raum had been my life—how could I hunt him down like a common criminal and deliver him into the hands of otherworldly justice?

But he *was* a criminal, albeit not a common one, and he deserved that justice.

"I'll speak with you, but I won't"—I motioned to his hands—"make any agreements."

His hands dropped to his sides, and he stared at me quite without expression. "Shall we?"

I didn't move. "I don't know your name."

He hesitated. To his species, giving one's name to a human gave power along with it. A name is a potent thing; with it you can call powers beyond your wildest imaginings, and you can define a being to your whim.

"He taught you the ancient tongue?"

"Yes. Enough of it to serve this purpose."

He named himself in the most ancient of human languages,

the one his kind claim Adam and Eve spoke. Using the primeval tongue was a tricky thing; your mind translated it into modern speech instantly and you were unable to recall the actual words spoken. You would always remember what you said in your own dialect, and the words would present themselves in images. His was joyful soaring . . . sun and moon . . . day and night . . . sincerity and arrogance . . .

"Surely not," I said with a trace of amusement, taking in his well-worn tee-shirt, faded jeans that were sprung at the knees, the dark stubble that shadowed a strong jaw. He looked like any other young man on the streets at night, edging inexorably from grunge to down-on-his-luck. Put a spray can in his hand and he'd be the epitome of the American graffiti artist.

"It's what your mind translated. I'm bound to you by that name now." He scuffed his sneaker on the sidewalk like a small boy, his tone speaking volumes on his opinion of my naming.

"Icarus it is. Did you fly too close to the sun, then?"

His eyes changed from ice blue to golden, copper brown. *Always showing off*, I thought with impatience—and not a little envy. If I could, I'd change the color of my eyes from espresso-bean brown to that gold he just affected—and no doubt he knew it.

"Not exactly. I've worked in the darkness so long that the sun seems far away now. Shall we take this to a café? You look like you could use a cup of coffee, and I wouldn't mind a hot chocolate."

I arched a brow at him, satisfied to see his species' version of a blush. His kind didn't need sustenance, but they *are* fond of certain human food and drink. "Certainly."

We found an all-night diner nearby and didn't speak again until coffee and cocoa were served. I took an experimental sip and made a face; coffee at an all-night greasy spoon was always a dicey proposition. But it wasn't too awful, and it was something for my hands to do. Lift, sip, lower. Lift, sip, lower. Lift . . .

"There have been eight victims," Icarus said. "Or maybe I should say there have been eight victims *found*. I'd be a fool to think there aren't more."

"Why is that?" I shifted uncomfortably in my chair. I didn't want to talk about *him*; he'd broken my heart, left me mourning for his unique brand of love, abandoned me to mediocrity after knowing otherworldly sensuality. Could anyone possibly blame me for indulging in a slice of bitter pie? I thought not.

"His arrogance is legendary, but so is his cleverness. And he would find it quite clever to hide the scope of his sins."

My fingers clenched around my coffee cup. "I can't help you hunt him. He was my lover."

His golden eyes dropped to my breast again, giving me the sensation that he could see through my blouse. Perhaps he could, although I'd never known x-ray vision to be one of their abilities.

"When one goes out of control, it is the obligation of one's . . . mate to bring justice," he replied, the forcefulness of his voice betraying deep emotion under his calm, cool exterior.

"He was my lover," I repeated numbly. "I adored him. He broke my heart. Sometimes I still . . . I still can't *breathe*, it hurts so much. How can you ask me to do this?"

Icarus met my gaze, sympathy darkening his eyes. As he stared, his form shifted, and for a sliver of a second, I saw his true shape. How could one *not* fall in love with these beings when one was fortunate—or unfortunate—enough to cross their paths?

"What did you name him?"

"No. I can't tell you that; you can find him through the name I gave him because I still have feelings for him. I'm smarter than that, Icarus."

"Suzanne," he said patiently. "Eight victims, probably more. Brutally murdered, torn limb from limb and partially eaten. You may have heard on the news that the coroner found saliva in the wounds of several of the victims. What you will never hear is that the saliva evidence has no DNA."

"That doesn't mean the perpetrator is of your species."

"Think," he said harshly, and rapped his finger painfully against my temple. "Do you know of any other species that could have done it and left behind saliva with no DNA?"

"Vampires? Werewolves?"

"Both will have DNA, albeit modified, because both are hybrid species, created from magic. Only angels have no DNA. Suzanne, you know this."

"There are more things under the sun than I will ever know," I replied stubbornly, avoiding his eyes.

He thrust his hands across the table in challenge, palms up, sending my coffee cup skidding over the edge of the table and into my lap. Thankfully the coffee was only lukewarm. I stared at his blank palms again; no life, love, or health lines.

"Suzanne, *please*," he whispered with desperation.

I battled the irresistible pull his kind has on mine, the desire that runs so deep it's part of time and the elements, something so base it defies explanation or definition.

Don't do it! Betrayal is betrayal, regardless of the circumstances.

His eyes mesmerized me; I could almost believe I was falling—falling out of my world and into his, falling under his persuasion.

Raum is killing people.

That fact couldn't be ignored, regardless of who—or what—brought the news to my ears. Only lack of common sense would allow me to willingly become involved with another *malakh*; despite this fact, I raised my hands and held them, trembling, just above his. He didn't move; it had to be my choice, this bond, and it could not be given lightly because once I touched my palms to his, we would be bonded for eternity. But to hunt my lover, I would need his protection, and bonding was the only way to gain it.

"What did you name him, Suzanne?"

"Raum."

His mouth fell open in shock and his hands jerked back as though he were reconsidering. I smacked my hands down on them, glaring at him defiantly. Heat seared where our skin touched, and then I felt a burning welt rise on my left breast. Shocked, I raised my gaze to his.

"What are you doing?" I whispered, horrified. "You marked my heart!" I didn't understand why—or how—he had done it.

"I'm sorry, Suzanne. It's the only way to protect you."

"But . . . to be able to do that, you have to . . . "

"You named him Raum, the Great Earl of Hell, the commander of thirty legions of demons. The invoker of love. Is it any wonder you've not been able to move on?"

I tried to stand up, but Icarus held my hands in an iron grip. "You had no right! You just bonded me as your wife! I can never have—oh my God!"

My voice trailed off as I realized just what he'd done. No white picket fence and two-point-five children and a husband—a human husband—who went to work at eight and came home at five every day. No, not for me—me, whose path had crossed not one but two of these wonderful, terrible creatures.

"We can discuss the finer points of what I've done later. For now, I think we've outstayed our welcome, and we have many things to discuss about . . . Raum."

"Icarus—"

"Yes, about that—for the sake of fewer explanations, let's just shorten it to Russ, shall we?"

He released my hands and scooted out of the booth, heading toward our waitress, who stared at us in shock and horror. She'd seen when Icarus—Russ—had that unguarded moment and let his true form show. She backed away from him as he approached, but there was nowhere for her to go; the counter was directly behind her and the stools were fixed to the floor. Trapped between them, she could only tremble with dread as he approached.

"I will not hurt you," he told her calmly. "But I can't allow you to remember that we were here." He touched her forehead with his first and middle fingers. "Forget the last hour. And sleep for two minutes."

Her eyes closed immediately. Russ took our ticket from her apron pocket, went to the register and opened it, and stuffed a five into a bill slot. A long pin held a stack of tickets, and he stabbed ours onto the top.

"That should take care of our tab and tip. She'll reconcile it up later, but she won't remember serving us. Let's go—we only have about thirty seconds."

That was time enough for us to vacate the café. Once on the street, I stopped.

"Ic—Russ. What do we do now?"

"We hunt Raum."

I fidgeted uncomfortably. That wasn't what I meant. "I mean about . . . well . . . the marriage bond."

He held my gaze for a long moment. "There's time enough to figure that out later. Let's go."

Russ strode off into the night, leaving me to follow or not. I could walk away or try to hide from him, but he could find me anywhere just by virtue of what he was. Now that he had marked me as a wife, he could find me with even greater ease.

After one last glance cast longingly back toward the café, I trotted after him, having to run partway to catch up with his longer strides. As I fell into step with him, his hand swung back and caught mine, and he twined our fingers together.

And that was how I married an angel.

Chapter Two

We walked for what seemed like hours—what had probably *been* hours, judging from the moon's progress across the sky. I knew I'd regret staying up all night.

"Where are we going? It's late; I need to sleep."

Russ stopped, tugging my hand to bring me to a halt beside him. "No time for sleep. We have much to discuss, such as Raum's favorite places, his daily habits. You know him best."

"No. God knows him best."

"He sent me to you."

I unwound my fingers from his, but he didn't let go of my hand. "I can't imagine why."

"Can't you," he replied, a statement rather than a question. "He sends you healing, Suzanne. Accept it."

"How is this healing? He wants me to betray my lover."

Russ's hand tightened for a fraction of a second. "He's no longer your lover." He began walking again, pulling me along behind him, ignoring my attempts to elicit a more logical response.

"What about my car?" I asked finally.

"We can't use it. It smells of you; he'll be able to find you, and through you, he'll find me."

"But—"

"We're going to neutral ground, and there I can shield you. He can trace you to there but not beyond."

"Neutral ground? Where would that be—a church?"

He spared me a purely human look of amusement. "A

church is hardly neutral."

We walked on, Russ in silence, me in annoyance. After another thirteen blocks, I tried to pull my hand away from his again. His fingers tightened.

"You don't want to do that, Suzanne," he said mildly.

"The hell I don't," I replied.

Without further argument, he let go. Instantly my whole body ached with fatigue and my trembling legs spilled me onto the sidewalk. Too late I realized that he'd been feeding me endurance through our linked flesh.

"Have I told you lately that I loathe your species?" I rubbed my calves, soothing weary muscles.

Russ knelt beside me. "I'll take that as sarcasm, because otherwise it's a lie. Here." A hand laid over one of mine stopped my makeshift massage. "It will take a little more effort now that you've broken the link."

"Kiss me and I'll put a stake through your heart."

He chuckled. "What heart? You know better."

His admonishment out of the way, he hauled me to my feet and wrapped me in an impossibly engulfing embrace. The full-body contact sent immediate relief singing through my muscles. When we started walking again, I felt refreshed and rejuvenated, and this time I didn't protest as he took my hand.

On we went, out of downtown Seattle and into Lower Queen Anne. Houses flashed by, both derelict and restored. I was mildly surprised to see a flip-flop from what I'd remembered: some of the more dilapidated abodes were now pristine, and some of my favorites, which I had jealously coveted, had gone to seed. Had it really been five years since I'd ventured into Queen Anne? There had been a bakery here I'd frequented in my life before Raum. I wondered if it was still there.

Thirty-six blocks into our thirty-eight block walk, it occurred to me where he was taking me. Not a church, because he was right—a church was hardly neutral. But there were other places where saints and sinners rubbed elbows in relative harmony.

Places such as Mount Pleasant Cemetery.

We wound our way between headstones across the carefully manicured lawns of the cemetery, heading deeper into the grounds away from the offices. The farther we went, the more uneasy I became; the seclusion was indicative of a need for privacy from prying eyes and ears. Just what did shielding entail? Raum had never done such a thing for me. I wondered suddenly whether it was because he had seen no need for it, or he had simply not cared if I had his protection.

Finally Russ stopped, turning to face me, still holding my hand. "You should sit for a moment before we start."

"Start *what*, exactly?" I gripped his hand tighter, resisting his gentle push to make me sit.

"The shielding. Suzanne, please—"

"This doesn't have anything to do with sex, does it? And the ground is wet, in case you hadn't noticed. This *is* Seattle." Raindrops glistened on the blades of grass, gleaming in the moonlight like tiny crystals.

"It's July; I doubt you'll succumb to hypothermia. And no, this has nothing to do with sex, so relax."

He wrenched his hand from mine and his gentle push became an inexorable shove toward the ground. The chilly rain soaked into the back of my slacks, and I sent him a reproachful look.

Russ knelt before me and held out his hands, palms up, waiting for me to lay mine upon them, his gaze steady as only an angel's could be. I hesitated.

"Do you trust me?" he asked quietly.

"Trust you?" I repeated incredulously. "I don't even know you!"

He didn't smile. "This is part of the process. Do you trust me? Don't say you do if you don't; that weakens my protection and we'll both be very sorry later."

Something in his tone made me think about his question

11

long and hard before I answered. Did I trust him, an angel who had accosted me on the street at night and shamed me into hunting my beloved? Could I even think of trusting another of the same species who had shown me the closest thing to heaven I'd ever know this side of death—as well as the most excruciating pain I could experience this side of hell?

I reflected that the fact I'd listened to him, and willingly left the café with him knowing why he sought me, spoke volumes more than my mere words could convey. Yes, I trusted him—trusted him enough, anyway—or I never would have come. Better yet, he never could have marked me with the marriage bond if I harbored any suspicions.

I laid my hands on his. Warm heat flowed from my fingertips, up through my arms, flooding my torso. His hands slid up the backs of my arms, spreading fiery heat in their wake. Not a sexual heat, but something infinitely more personal and binding. I felt it coil through my blood, invading my very DNA, and belatedly I wondered just what I was allowing myself to be drawn into. From the moment Raum crashed into my life—literally—I'd known nothing but extremes: exhilaration, unbounded joy, despair, and darkest depression. Insanity was the only explanation for allowing another of his kind this level of familiarity.

My whole body tingled as though an electrical current thrummed through my nerve endings. Every molecule of my being came vibrantly alive. I felt as though I could scale the tallest buildings and embrace the world.

"Don't try to stand yet," Russ cautioned as I lurched to my knees. The surge of energy through my limbs made me awkward and shaky. "The intensity will pass in a moment, and you'll be able to handle yourself with coordination."

"How long can you keep up a shield like this?"

"Indefinitely. That was the purpose of the marriage bond— in addition to hiding you from him."

"But what about—"

"No time to talk about that now, Suzanne. And speaking of

12

. . . " He leaned away from me, still balanced on his haunches, and surveyed me with a critical eye. "I can't keep calling you that. We're going to have to find another name for you."

"Crazy?" I suggested, tongue firmly in cheek.

Russ surprised me by cracking a smile. "While perhaps it's apt, it's not very flattering for such an attractive woman."

I thought for a moment. "My best friend in high school was named Zanna. Everyone called us Sue-Zanna when we were together. You know, a play on the name Susanna?"

"I'm an angel, not an idiot," he replied. "How well does Raum know her?"

"He's never met her. I don't think I even mentioned her while we were together."

"She's not your best friend anymore?"

"She stopped speaking to me during our last year of college."

"Let me guess: a man." He straightened, holding his hands down to help me up. "No, I don't think we can use that. You'll have a lot of emotions about it, even if they're buried deep. He'll have seen them."

I scowled at him. "It's really complicated being involved with your species. Can you see now why I wanted nothing to do with this?"

"You think your species is a picnic?" he countered calmly. "Always finding trouble even while we're working hard to keep you out of it."

I pulled my hands away, only now realizing he was still holding them. "If I'd had a guardian angel, he would have kept me from becoming involved with Raum. Therefore, I must conclude from the events of the last few years that I was either not assigned one, or he abandoned his post."

"He looked away at a crucial moment. Believe me, he is regretful." He twitched his shoulders back, as though flexing wings. "It's not as effective as physical contact, but as long as I'm shielding you, I can feed you strength without touching you. I'm sure that will please you."

"Immensely."

"I think I'll call you Bree."

If he meant to throw me off balance with the sudden change in topic, he was going to have to do better than that. "Bree? Why Bree?"

"In the ancient Scots language, it means a disturbance. I think it's suitable."

"Ha ha."

But he was already shaking his head. "No, I'll never remember to call you that. We'll just have to trust that we won't attract attention using your real name."

"Now what do we do?"

"Now we find a hole we can crawl into so we can talk."

"I'll need to sleep sometime."

Russ stared at me silently for a long moment, and then pulled his lower lip between his teeth, chewing on it thoughtfully. I wondered from what human he'd picked this up; perhaps the same one from whom he'd learned to love hot chocolate.

"You need less rest now than you ordinarily would, but you're right. Eventually you'll need to sleep. Otherwise, when I withdraw the shield, you'll collapse from exhaustion."

"That's an uplifting thought. I have enough problems right now without adding hospitalization to the mix."

"You have problems you never even dreamed of, Suzanne. Come, let's find a place to hole up, and I'll tell you all about them."

A hand at my back urged me forward, and I slanted a look up at him as we crept out of the cemetery. Well, *I* crept; Russ moved with preternatural silence, as though not even the twigs in the grass dared obey the laws of physics by snapping under his weight.

"I'm beginning to suspect you play a large part in those problems," I said.

"You've no idea."

We navigated our way out of Queen Anne and started the long walk to parts unknown. After several blocks, he offered his arm. After a couple more, I took hold of it. A while later, I ventured to speak.

"Are we going to walk all night? Can't you just . . . fly us somewhere?"

"He lied to you about that. It doesn't work that way."

"He lied to me about a lot of things." Such as he loved me. And that he would never leave me. And that he could fly. And that . . .

"Hey, is it true that you can vanish from here and appear in Venice in an instant?"

Russ sighed expressively. Another lie, apparently.

On we walked, through Southeast Magnolia and into Briarcliff and finally, at long last, to a deserted strip of beach at the edge of Puget Sound where we took refuge amongst a clutter of driftwood.

"Lie down and sleep," Russ advised softly. "Plenty of time to talk after morning breaks."

I lay down in the sand without argument, shivering at the chill of night held in the grains of shell, rock, and silica. He sat cross-legged beside me, offering his lap for a pillow. I accepted, but I didn't sleep right away. A blush of lighter blue and pink tinged the eastern sky, fading to the indigo of deep night in the west.

I watched the stars as they faded one by one with the coming dawn and fell asleep wondering what this new day would bring.

Chapter Three

"I feel like I haven't eaten in days." I stretched and yawned, making a production of it to cover my embarrassment at having awakened with my face pressed firmly against his abdomen, my mouth precarious inches from an indecent position.

"You've done a lot of walking," Russ replied, oblivious to my discomfiture.

The sand was warm beneath me, the sky grey, but the air pleasant. I blinked, clearing my bleary eyes, and looked around. The beach looked different by the light of day; there was less driftwood scattered about than I remembered stumbling over the previous night. The tide was out, giving more depth to the strip of sand between the road and the water's edge. A flock of gulls huddled at the edge of the surf, rushing in as the waves rolled out in search of crab and sand dollars and other morsels left behind.

"Is this the same beach?" I blurted, glaring at him suspiciously.

He shrugged. "It looks different in the daylight," he echoed my earlier thought. "I burned some of the driftwood to keep you warm while I went to find you food."

"You left me here alone, asleep? Are you insane?"

He frowned. "Suzanne, you were perfectly safe. I have you shielded; no one would ever have found you. Here— you'll feel better once you eat."

He had already opened the package he handed me.

Peppered beef jerky—not my normal fare for breakfast, but I wasn't going to complain. While I chewed on a thick strip, he rummaged in a plastic grocery sack and brought out a bottle of cran-raspberry juice, which he uncapped and set in the sand next to me.

"Where are we going today? Do you have any idea where Raum is hiding?"

He didn't answer; he fiddled with the remaining contents of the grocery bag, then stared out at the surf crashing and rolling up on the beach.

I asked more urgently, "Russ, do you know where he is?"

His eyes moved to my face, and their color shifted from blue to a rich, earthy brown. "No. But . . . there was another murder last night. Same characteristics."

My mind went utterly blank. The two bites of jerky I'd consumed churned in my stomach. And then my panicked heart denied the truth of his words. It couldn't be—Raum couldn't have sunk so far into depravity in three short years— well, short for him. Time dragged out for me, being human, but three years was but a blip in the stream of time to his kind. I was positive that while I had been with him, there had been no indication of a capacity for such evil.

"I'm sorry, Suzanne. I know how hard this will be for you, but I'd like to head to the scene of the last murder."

"Oh, Russ, I don't see the point—"

"Eat up," he interrupted, but gently. His expression was kind. "We have a long walk ahead of us." And he said no more.

We skirted Elliot Bay Marina and followed the trail to Myrtle Edwards Park. He led the way to a patch of grass near the water, where it would be harder for anyone to hear our conversation over the surf—not that anyone approached us. There were a surprising number of people wandering the park, considering the grey day—well, perhaps not so surprising for Seattle; if you waited for a clear day to engage in outdoor activities, you would never go out. No one paid attention to us even when they passed by so close I could feel the breath of air in their wake.

"Sit, eat," he commanded. He let go of my arm as my backside touched ground, and exhaustion flooded through me. We had only walked a couple of miles, but I knew it wasn't physical activity that dragged at my limbs. Despair and depression, held at bay only when Russ loaned me his energy, dragged me down and encouraged me to stay there forever.

We didn't speak while I finished the bag of peppered jerky and washed it down with juice. Russ held on to the grocery bag, obviously intending to dole out my sustenance throughout the day. I wondered what else he'd bought; angels weren't known for keeping up on the necessities of human nutrition, although I couldn't deny that the jerky gave me protein and the juice some necessary vitamins.

When I crumpled the jerky package, he turned to sit cross-legged in front of me. "We must discuss Raum. I know it's going to be difficult for you, but if you can remember all the places he favored, we may stand a chance of finding him before he hurts someone else."

"I can't remember everywhere he liked to go. It was a long time ago. Unlike your species, I don't have an infallible memory."

"Just the places you can remember will do, Suzanne," he assured me, glancing around to check the proximity of the other park dwellers and whether they had overheard him.

I frowned, thinking backward in time. There were favorite restaurants—angels can process food with no trouble, and Raum certainly had enjoyed Italian cuisine. But his favorite place was an exclusive Hungarian *étterem*.

"Where is this restaurant?" Russ asked when I mentioned it.

"Down near Pike's Place Market." I pinched the bridge of my nose between my thumb and forefinger, trying to quiet a stress headache. Or perhaps it was a hunger headache. "Is there more to eat in that bag? More protein?"

He reached in without looking and handed me a huge plastic jar of cashews. "What else do you remember?"

"He knew the proprietor." I wrested off the lid and scooped up a handful of nuts. They crunched satisfyingly between my teeth. "But while he was at ease with the man, the man didn't appear to quite trust Raum. He always gave the impression that he'd rather Raum not come in."

"Does he know that Raum is an angel?"

"No clue. We never spoke about him. I don't know if Raum ever had any contact with the man outside of our dining experiences. He frequented the aquarium as well. He said he liked to watch the fish swim but wished they were in the sea."

I smiled wistfully and felt the smile pull into a grimace of sorrow. If Russ noticed, he didn't mention it.

"Keep going," he encouraged.

"Aahh . . . some coffee shop a few blocks from Waterfront Park. I can't remember the name; something Spanish, I think."

"Oh yes, he went there often," Russ said, nodding.

"How did you know that?"

"Raum and I met there occasionally."

My narrow-eyed gaze took in his bland expression but found no trace of deceit. "He never mentioned you."

He offered a slight shrug, another human affectation. "No reason why he would. They were not pleasant meetings."

I let the silence spin out between us, laden with my unspoken question, until he relented.

"Very well. I was sent to convince him to come back into obedience."

The cashews suddenly felt like sawdust in my mouth. I swallowed with difficulty. "Convince him to leave me, you mean. Well, you succeeded. Congratulations."

"I didn't succeed, Suzanne," he said with a trace of anger. "He stayed with you until he could no longer overcome his compulsion to murder. I'm just grateful he didn't choose you as his first victim."

"Often, serial murderers don't harm a significant other," I

pointed out. "Look at Robert Yates in Spokane. Never harmed his family."

"And often, family are a serial killer's first victims," he countered. "Ronald Gene Simmons in Arkansas and Mark Barton in Georgia."

Conceding his point with a wave of my hand, I munched more cashews, mulling over the events of the last eighteen hours. Too many things didn't add up, but that was only my heart talking. I didn't want Raum to be a murderer; that I hadn't known the depravity of which he was capable after the unparalleled intimacy we'd shared meant I was a lousy judge of character. And yes, it also meant that there would be no reconciliation with my otherworldly lover, no reparation to my heart unless Russ could heal my emotions like he could strengthen my body.

"Why am I so tired? I thought you could feed me strength without touching me since the shielding, but when you let go of me . . . "

"I'm trying not to let you rely too much on my abilities. You'll become addicted—as you did with Raum—and it will be harder when I leave."

For some reason, the thought of Russ leaving stung. He was my only connection to the angelic world, the only chance to experience wonders and abilities beyond my human reality. And then, for an instant, I imagined how my life might be had I not seen Raum as he came in for a landing on the roof of my building; had he not been startled by my exclamation and crashed, wounding his wing; had I not obliged him as nursemaid while he healed, and then as lover.

Might I have married the man I'd been dating when I met Raum, the man whom I had found perfectly delightful until he had been eclipsed by an angel? Might I be holding the children I'd always wanted—the children I would never have now that I was marked with the marriage bond of a *malakh*?

"Who else can you remember with whom Raum might have had more than a casual acquaintance?"

"Before I recite his earthly phonebook, perhaps you can give me some information first."

"Such as?" Although he was unperturbed, tension shifted his posture until he strongly resembled one of his marble brethren.

"The marriage bond. First, I don't understand how you were able to do it. Second, I don't understand *why* you did it when you know what it means for me, for my future."

Russ tied the plastic grocery bag closed and tucked it into the space between his folded legs. He leaned toward me, and his eyes turned the depthless blue of a cloudless summer sky. His expression was grave.

"What do you know about the marriage bond?"

I offered a half-shrug. "Only what Raum told me. He refused to mark me with it"—I sent him a reproachful look—"not only because it's forbidden but because he said he didn't want me to never be able to go on if something happened to him. He said things like that a lot: 'If something happens to me, Suzanne.' Sometimes he acted like he was being hunted. He was never fully at ease."

"He wasn't being hunted, but he was being hounded—by me," Russ reminded me. "If someone else was after him, I don't know about it."

"Maybe he only left me to keep me safe."

"Suzanne," he said patiently, "he left you, period. Not only did he leave, he left you unprotected. Thank God that He sent me or who knows what might have gotten to you first."

I scowled, not pleased that he had deflated my bubble of hope so easily. "Anyway, he told me about the different kinds of bonds. The kind he had with me—"

"A sexual bond," he broke in.

My scowl turned into a full-fledged glower. "Yes," I agreed sharply. A faint smile touched his mouth. "As I was saying, the kind of bond he had with me was the most common. It marked me as his, provided me with a means to call for help if I desperately needed it, and was least intrusive on my humanity."

"And yet you can't move on."

"And *then* there's the marriage bond," I plowed on with cold contempt. "The most binding of all, that links me to the otherworld for the remainder of my life, that will repel all human males, that will render me barren to human seed. You should not have been able to do it. It's prohibited."

"It was allowed in this instance."

"Why?"

"So I could more fully protect you. You will never move on; you've already shown that. Three years—human years—is time enough for heartache to ease and your attention to move on to human men. And yet you haven't. So I was told to do as I must, and the marriage bond was not only permitted but encouraged. I must protect you."

"Why? I'm only one human."

The twist of Russ's mouth was less of a smile than it was a grimace of sorrow. "Do you think God cares only for the collective? He would leave the flock to seek out one lamb. You're that lamb, Suzanne. Now please, tell me about anyone else you remember with whom Raum may have had more than casual contact. Anyone for whom he might have harbored affection."

Glad to abandon the subject of irrevocable bonds to the heavenly realm, I racked my brain to think of people whom Raum might've mentioned, and he never mentioned anyone unless he held them in higher than average esteem.

"There was the clerk at the grocery store—what was her name? Andrea, I think. That librarian he liked—oh, her name's Debbie. Annoying woman. A gas station attendant he said was brilliant; that was Jordan. He's not there anymore, just quit coming in to work."

"Jordan is more than likely dead," Russ said bluntly. "I

suspect he's been murdered and hidden to cover the scope of Raum's activity."

"Oh." I couldn't think of anything else to say.

"Let's go through your list so far. The restaurant's proprietor is still living, but Raum's favorite server, a young man named Emil, was the fourth victim found. An attendant at the aquarium, a middle-aged grandmother-to-be, was the fifth victim. The clerk at the grocery store Raum frequented was victim number six. Debbie, the annoying librarian—victim number seven. A barista from the espresso shop, a beautiful young woman—victim number eight. Three others—the first three—you might or might not have known, but Raum almost certainly did."

"He's killing people he knew," I murmured, shocked by this more than anything else. "Why would he do that? They trusted him, liked him."

"That was his plan. Make them comfortable with him, and it's easier to lure them to a private location where he can kill them."

The cashews threatened to bolt back up my esophagus. I screwed the cap back onto the jar and shoved them at Russ, who put them back in the bag without comment. I stared out at the surf crashing against the breakfront. A few intrepid kayakers skimmed along the surface of Elliot Bay, safely clad in wetsuits against the chill of the choppy water.

"There's more, Suzanne," he said after a moment, his voice quiet. "The murder last night . . . "

"It was someone Raum knew. Someone I knew, too?"

"I'm sorry," he whispered and took my hands, gently holding them between us. "Zanna is dead."

It took a moment for his words to make sense. The words "Zanna who?" hovered on the tip of my tongue and then died there as at last I comprehended. Zanna, my best friend in high school and college, with whom I had parted ways over the man I had left for Raum. How had he known about her? I'd never mentioned her. Of that I was sure, because mentioning her would have meant telling him why our friendship had fallen apart, and that was something I would never have done.

And then what Russ wasn't saying slowly gelled in my mind. The progression of victims was a story in itself: from people only he knew to people we both knew—and now to people only I knew. Although I silently willed him not to, he said the words I dreaded to hear spoken aloud.

"He's coming after you, Suzanne."

Chapter Four

I couldn't look at him as I talked; instead, I stared into the flames, watching them lick at the midnight sky with greedy tongues of orange and green.

"I used to be able to run for miles without getting tired or winded."

My voice, pitched low, was barely audible over the crackle of the driftwood fire. I didn't care if he heard me. This was my confession to the night, to the ocean, to the wind. To God.

Despair wasn't the only reason I avoided his gaze; embarrassment kept my eyes averted. How pitiful I must be to his species; how unimaginative, how limited. No wonder Raum had left; his disdain for my human frailty must have slid inexorably into disgust.

"And *strong* . . . Lord, was I strong."

Heavy loads had been feather-light, and my legs had been able to propel me to the roof of a one-story house. I'd only needed four hours of sleep each night and could eat anything, and as much as I wanted. Often I knew things about people from a simple touch of their hand, and could influence a person's decisions with a concentrated thought directed at him or her.

But beyond those things had been that feeling of being special, chosen. An angel had chosen me—*me*, Suzanne Harper—over all the other humans on earth, and had shared with me some of his extraordinary abilities. I'd come as close as anyone ever would to knowing what it was like to be one of the *malakhim*.

"He was dating her first. She was certain he was The One, so she wanted me to meet him."

Oh, how excited Zanna had been to have two of her favorite people meet and become friends. Had she noticed the instant electricity between Ian and me, the force like two magnets propelling us toward each other? No, I rather doubted she had. She had been too wrapped up in her own happiness to see the vibrant attraction that had flared between us. And hadn't there been a part of me that had justified that attraction because I was the more beautiful of us two? Yes, there was no doubt that I had.

"You stole him," Russ surmised with his usual uncomfortable bluntness.

I closed my eyes, mortification burning my cheeks a brilliant red, horrified at his blunt deduction. "I stole him."

"So Zanna had every reason not to speak to you all these years."

"Yes. I justified it because I thought Zanna was plain, and since I was more attractive I deserved a man like Ian Reid. She could go find someone else who fit her looks. I thought that and a lot more."

Tears crept down my cheeks. Neither of us mentioned them. I had harbored this guilt deep in my heart for eight years—the three years I'd spent with Ian, and the five years since I'd left him for Raum. Now Zanna was dead, and I would never have the chance to tell her how wrong I'd been, how sorry I was for what I'd done, how much I had missed her.

A sob escaped my clamped lips. I plastered a hand over my mouth, but nothing would hold back my grief. Too late, too late—I'd come to repentance too late to make any difference. She was gone forever, gone beyond my shame and sorrow, beyond her anger and bitterness. Beyond my ability to hurt her anymore.

His arm slid around me, and he pulled me against him, his

hand pressing my cheek to his chest. My tears flowed over it in an unrelenting stream. He offered no trite words of comfort, and I was glad for it. Zanna was dead because of me, and she had died with her heart broken by my actions. I deserved no comfort.

A long while later I sat hiccupping into Russ's silent chest, my tears dried by the heat from the fire. His hand still cradled my face, and with furtive guilt I took comfort from its warm pressure.

"Sleep, Suzanne," he murmured, and with relief I let consciousness swirl away and sank gratefully into oblivion.

* * *

The sun was wrong when I next opened my eyes. At first I couldn't place why, and then I realized it hung in the sky more to the west than the east. I'd slept through the night and most of the day. My head was pillowed on a plastic shopping bag draped over a mound of sand. Russ sat motionless a few feet away, watching the surf crash onto the shore. Gulls wheeled overhead; the wind carried their shrieks away from the sea, making them sound deceptively distant. I wondered vaguely if they'd managed to crap on any part of my body as I lay here in the shade of a pile of driftwood.

"No, the shielding protects you from bird crap too," Russ said distractedly.

"How'd you know I was thinking that?"

"You were talking in your sleep a while ago." He finally turned to look at me, offering a troubled smile. "We should get going. I had planned on going to Zanna's yesterday, but I guess I've been driving you too hard. You needed the sleep."

"Is something wrong, Russ?"

He shrugged. "I've been hunting him for so long, I can't believe I'm so close."

29

I sat up and stretched. Midway through a jaw-cracking yawn, I realized what he'd said. "I thought you didn't know where he is."

"Poor choice of words," he replied, frowning. He turned, scattering sand across my jeans. Frustration made his voice a tight growl. "I know where he's been. I just can't anticipate where he'll be next."

"Why does this fall to you, anyway? If he knows you're hunting him, why isn't someone else—someone he doesn't suspect—sent after him?"

"It's my purpose. All angels have responsibilities. Some are sent to watch over the humans. Others watch over the other angels. Yet others, like me, are fallen angel hunters—not a pleasant job—and there aren't that many of us."

"He's fallen?"

Russ made an impatient sound. "He's murdering people, Suzanne. Of course he's fallen, but not in the terms you're thinking of. He's not one of the original rebellion. I've been a watcher, over both humans and angels. Now I'm called to be a hunter. But he's just always one step ahead of me." His hand clenched into a tight fist, pressing into the flesh of his thigh.

My stomach growled, ending his introspection. He rummaged in the grocery bag beside him and handed me the jar of cashews. I screwed off the top and dove in. His odd, distracted demeanor faded into the background as I chomped my way through a quarter of the nuts left in the jar. When the hunger pangs abated, he silently handed me a bottle of juice. The juice barely slaked my thirst.

"Is there a bottle of water in there? I'm really thirsty."

"No, but we can get some on our way to Zanna's."

I bit my lip. "Explain again why we have to go there."

"I'm hoping he left some sort of clue that will lead me to him."

"He's been too smart to make a mistake like that."

"If he left a clue, it wouldn't be by mistake. It would be a challenge to me to find him. I have to take the risk of him laying a trap for me. Are you ready? Have you rested enough?"

I nodded, gathering my trash. We'd spent the night on a strip of beach with parking and other amenities. I was amazed we hadn't been rousted and run off during the night. As we passed a trash receptacle, I smiled hesitantly at the girl standing next to it. She stared at my left eyebrow and then turned away without a change in expression. I raised a brow at Russ, but he only tugged me toward the sidewalk.

We walked with steadfast determination, mostly silent. Residential neighborhoods and business corridors flowed by in a steady stream, blending seamlessly into a blur of familiar haunts and unrecognized venues, the latter of which signaled more lost pieces of a past too painful to dwell on.

Russ held my hand in a loose grip, feeding me strength to keep exhaustion at bay. We stopped to rest on the edge of Rizal Park, and he waited until we were lounging on the grassy edge of the park to let go of my hand. Weariness flooded through me in an instant. I was only vaguely aware of leaning heavily against his shoulder, and of him easing me down to pillow my head in his lap.

The sun was nearly set when I woke, staining the clouds in a glorious display of crimson, orange, and gold. I stretched and sat up, my stomach gurgling.

Russ glanced at me, amused. "Hungry already?"

"Unlike you," I replied tartly, "I have to eat every few hours."

"I forget sometimes." He rummaged in the plastic grocery sack and tossed me a bag of teriyaki jerky. "That should tide you over."

"Much more walking, Russ, and I'm going to need new jeans." In just the three days since I'd met him, my jeans had started to fit loosely. I was going to need a real meal soon. Saliva flooded my mouth at the thought of a hearty

31

dinner of roasted chicken and baby reds and—

"We're almost done, I think."

I paused midway through biting a thick piece of jerky in half. "Done? Is he close?"

"*Closer*," he stressed. "I think we're right to go to Zanna's. He feels stronger." He trailed into silence for a long time.

"He feels stronger? What do you mean?"

"We leave behind a trace of our presence everywhere we go. That trace gets stronger the closer we get to each other. I can feel him now; I just can't pinpoint him." The edge of frustration in his steely voice made me glad he wasn't hunting me.

"And then what? You're going to confront him after he's murdered God knows how many people? Are you crazy?"

He quirked a funny little smile in my direction. "Insanity is an affliction of your species but never mine."

"You can't call what he's doing the actions of a sane being," I argued.

"Not sane as you define it." In human terms, in other words, with our limited understanding and penchant for filing everyone away in tidy little boxes with definitive labels.

"But—"

"Suzanne," he broke in with a trace of impatience. "We're good or we're bad. It's as simple as that. Acts of depravity amongst the fallen don't indicate a lack of sanity, just a lack of regard for morality."

"I still think—"

"You want some comfort in the face of what he's done, and I can understand that. But you can't let that desire blind you to reality. He's completely aware of what he's doing, and he made a deliberate decision to do it."

I subsided into silence, stung by his sharpness. Was I wrong to hope against all hope that we were wrong, that it was some other angel murdering humans and framing Raum for it?

"I'm sorry," he said finally, his tone conciliatory. "I didn't mean to be so harsh. I'm just afraid that if you get your hopes too high that I'm wrong about him, you're going to be hurt exponentially when I'm proven right."

"Maybe you won't be."

He favored me with a pitying look. "I have it on the highest authority. He's the angel responsible. Finish your jerky. We still have another hour or so of walking."

I needed no further encouragement. I fell to my meal with gusto, and in short order had polished off the jerky, leaving nothing to show for my meal but slightly sticky fingers. He handed me another bottle of juice, and I was relieved to see that this time it was grape. I had developed a distaste for cran-raspberry juice over the last two days.

"Feeling better?"

"Much."

"Onward, then."

We started out again, and as we rounded the corner onto Rainier Avenue, I slipped my hand into his. He looked down with a surprised smile but made no comment. His fingers squeezed mine, and we walked in comfortable stride.

Our route was a long, a straight walk down Rainier Avenue to South Genesee. Zanna lived—had lived—at the south end of the park on a quiet, pleasant street. I paused at the end of the back walk, unable to look away from the blaring yellow crime scene tape that barred our way. Russ ducked under it.

"We can't go in there. It's still a crime scene."

He arched a brow. "Sure we can."

"Someone's going to see us and call the police. How will you explain that?"

"No one will see us."

Still I hesitated, skeptical, and he retraced his steps. His hands came to rest on my shoulders, and his eyes shifted from cool blue to almost copper, as though he knew it was my favorite and sought to comfort me.

"Suzanne, haven't you wondered why no one stopped

while we were sitting for so long at the side of Dearborn Street? Or why no one bothered you on the beach when I went to get you food? No one can see us."

"Really?" I wasn't so sure I liked that idea. What if something happened to him? Would the shielding break, and I'd become visible again? Or would I be condemned to wander through a world where no one could see me?

"The marriage bond and the shielding will break if anything happens to me," Russ said; his fingers tightened a fraction. "Don't worry. Now, do you want to stay out here while I look around inside?"

I glanced at the door. "Is it . . . do you think it's really bad?"

His eyes darkened. "Yes, I think it's *very* bad."

"I'll stay out here, then. I don't think I can . . ."

His hands fell away, and without another word he pivoted and strode away from me. The locked doorknob was no match for otherworldly abilities. He gained easy access, and he didn't look back as he stepped across the threshold. The house swallowed him.

I sat in the grass beside the patio, ignoring the comfortable deck chairs under the shade of the awning. Zanna had not welcomed me here when she had been alive; I wasn't going to make myself at home just because she wasn't here to object. The lawn needed to be mowed; my fingers cropped all that was within reach in an effort to distract my mind from what was in the house.

The sun warmed my shoulders. I stared at my arms so I wouldn't have to look at the streak of crimson on the door trim. My skin had turned a lovely shade of brown. I hadn't been this tan in years, since I'd had the time—and the inclination—to sunbathe. It generally took several weeks of dedicated sun worshipping to achieve this shade.

I frowned, thinking back over the time since I'd met Russ. Had it only been three days? It felt like much longer. With my weight loss and tanned skin, it was almost easy to believe it *had* been longer. And there were stretches of time that I couldn't remember passing, one moment being aware of the sun burning down from one angle, and the next it shone from a direction it should have passed hours before.

I wondered if my jumbled memory had something to do with Russ feeding me his strength; I slept so deeply that upon waking I had several moments of complete amnesia. *Angels*, I grumbled silently. *Damn angels.*

I glanced up, checking the back door to see if he was coming out yet. The door, open just a crack, beckoned to me, enticing me. *Come see what he did to her, the girl you learned to drive with; the girl you first drank whiskey with— and puked with; the girl who followed you from California to Seattle to go to a college she hated just to be near you; the girl whose man you stole and whose heart you broke. Come see the end of the heartbreak, splattered across the white walls Zanna so favored. Come see what waits ahead for you when Raum finally gets around to you.*

I blinked the thought away, surprised to find myself on the back porch, pushing the door open.

He had caught her in the kitchen. The Mexican floor tiles were stained with a large, sticky puddle of blood that had been left to dry. The walls were not white, but a warm butter yellow with crimson splatters that might have been artful had they been paint rather than blood. They were darker than I'd expected, more russet than red. The scent hung thick and bitter in the air, closed up as the house had been. Zanna had no family, and separated from Ian and me, there was no one to call for a crime scene clean-up. Her house, paid for long ago through an insurance settlement, would remain empty until unpaid property taxes forced the county to sell the parcel at auction or a will transferred the deed to someone she'd found deserving.

I dragged my eyes away from the bloody floor. A newspaper lay open on the table, sprinkled with scarlet drops. I could just make out part of a headline: *Police call off search for missing—*

"Suzanne," Russ said with concern.

I hadn't realized I was headed toward the floor until he caught me. He pressed my face to his chest and carried me outside, where I lay with my cheek against the cool blades of grass for a long time.

An ant crawled up a long, broad blade, wavered at the tip, and lumbered back down. I watched it zigzag across the dead thatch under the green lawn until it disappeared. Still I stared until I realized something else was in the thatch. A tarnished circle of cheap metal with a die-cut heart, mashed into the dirt. Ian had worn one like it when we were living together; we'd bought a matching pair at some little stand at the fair after indulging in too many funnel cakes. The heart on his had been cut funny, a little lopsided.

I pushed my fingers through the thatch and pried the ring from the ground, brushing the soil out of a lopsided heart.

My heart hammered against my ribs so hard I thought it might burst from my chest. I sat up slowly, a scream of anguish building in my throat, my heart plummeting into a bottomless chasm of shock and misery. *No. Oh no no no, not this, anything but this!*

"Suzanne?" Russ queried sharply.

I raised my face to the sun and screamed, and screamed again.

Russ pressed his hand to my forehead, and I knew no more.

Chapter Five

"Suzanne, you have to eat." To tempt me, he waved a fragrant piece of jerky beneath my nose, but I turned away.

"What's the point?"

"Survival," Russ said simply.

I closed my eyes, easing their dry, gritty ache. "Again I ask, what's the point?"

He didn't answer. Instead of pressing my point, I eased myself down into the grass, warmed by the fair summer day, and curled into a ball. We had arrived at this park while I had been unconscious. Russ had only briefly explained that we were going to Ian's house; I didn't recognize the tiny but well-kept square of recreational land. Trees dotted the flat landscape, offering shade on rare days when the sun beat down without mercy. Traffic was slow on the street that flanked it, and from behind us came the sound of water and boats.

I *think* we were in the Montlake neighborhood—the area was upscale, the lawns manicured, the houses just a bit larger than necessary. Fresh out of college, Ian had gone to work for the Navy as an administrative assistant, and he'd lived modestly for a number of years, socking away most of his salary in his savings account and long-term certificates of deposit. He could afford to live here, although he'd always preferred to live in smaller, cheaper accommodations, such as my cozy apartment in Seward Park.

When he moved out of my apartment, I had no idea

where he planned to go. His packing had been done in bitter silence after a savage argument. The parting words he'd given me on his way out the door, the last of his belongings stuffed into a box and held carelessly under one arm, had been surprisingly gentle.

"There's something not right about him, Suze. You let me know when you figure out what." In Ian-speak, that translated to *I'll be here when things fall apart with him.*

No, I hadn't known to where he'd moved, but he'd never changed his phone number. I knew that because he called me every Christmas and birthday, and Caller ID doesn't lie.

The terrible thought that I'd never get another of those calls was too much to bear. I curled up into a tighter ball, wishing the sun could chase away the chill in my heart that sank into my very bones. Ian had been at Zanna's, his ring was crushed into the dirt under the thick carpet of green grass, and my mind could put two and two together with remarkable, graphic ease: he was dead, and for reasons known only to his killer, he had been hidden so he wasn't discovered when Zanna was found.

His killer. Raum.

A hand smoothed down my back, and warmth and strength flooded through me. Russ. Russ and his damnable otherworldly powers. My life had been ruined by his kind; I didn't need his comfort or concern. I shrugged away from his hand, perversely welcoming back the chill, the fierce ache in muscle and bone, the gnawing hunger and persistent thirst.

"I'm only trying to help."

"Famous last words."

He frowned. "What do you mean?"

"Those are the very same words I said to Ian when Raum crashed on my roof and I mended him." Something bothered me about this, but I was too weary to chase it down.

"I'm sure you meant well. You couldn't have known what you were getting into."

"It's no excuse," I said flatly.

A shadow fell between me and the sunlight. I opened my eyes to find Russ's face close to mine. His eyes shifted from blue to brown and settled somewhere near hazel.

"We're almost done, Suzanne. Raum is close, I can feel him. And when it's all settled and he's dealt with, I can take away the memory of all of this."

"You can do that?"

"Yes. It's generally how we handle these . . . situations when they happen."

I considered the very tempting offer. To forget the last five years since the *malakhim* had intruded in my life would be heaven. But would it change an essential part of who I was? I didn't want to lose identity; I just wanted relief from the unrelenting longing and sorrow.

"It's a kind offer," I murmured, "but more than I deserve. Should we go?"

"Once you eat," he said firmly. He pulled me upright and shoved the bag of beef jerky into my hands. I hesitated only briefly, considering refusing, but again—what was the point? Placate him until we went our separate ways, and then I could wallow in my misery until hunger or thirst ended it.

Because I knew what he wouldn't admit: Ian was dead. His ring had been mashed into the ground in Zanna's back yard, which meant he'd been there. Wearing it. Dying with Zanna. Because of me.

And now we were going to Ian's house, and I knew we would find either Raum or his last lure, leading us into his snare to live or die. I didn't care which.

While I ate, he uncapped a bottle of Gatorade and set it by my knee. I wrinkled my nose, but I would drink it. It was full of electrolytes and God knew this trek around Seattle was taking its toll on me. Abruptly I stopped gnawing on the thin sheet of dried, teriyaki-flavored beef.

"You shielded me so he can't find me. So why aren't we taking the bus or a taxi? Why are we walking?"

"The most safety I can provide is to make you invisible. It would be quite a trick to catch a cab or a bus when no one can see us. How could we get the cab driver to take us where we want to go? What would the bus driver think when his door won't close after the last passenger he can see boards? Or the other passengers when the seemingly vacant space before them is impassable?"

"I see your point." Losing interest, I went back to the jerky, methodically chewing through what was left in the bag without tasting it. I reluctantly chased it with the Gatorade, making faces as I swallowed but knowing I needed it. When I was done, he gathered my trash while I stood up and brushed the grass from my jeans. My clean, brand new jeans. For the first time I realized the shirt I wore was clean and smelled new.

"You changed my clothes," I said, a note of accusation sharpening my tone.

"You were very sick after we left Zanna's house," he said carefully. "I didn't think you would want to walk around Seattle in vomit-splattered clothing."

I flushed. "I don't remember that, but you're right. I wouldn't have wanted to do that. But . . . I don't know. It just seems a little . . . creepy." Perverted, more like.

"I've seen naked human women before. You have nothing I want, Suzanne."

"So unlike others of your kind, you don't find us humans attractive?"

"Of course you're attractive. I just have more control over myself than others of my species. Let's go, Suzanne. We don't have far to walk this time."

We crossed the park and turned north on the first street we came to. I didn't pay attention to the street signs until the road curved west and became East Shelby Street. I knew where we were now; definitely the Montlake neighborhood. On the other side of the houses to our right was the Montlake Cut, a manmade waterway connecting Portage Bay to Union Bay. If

40

we turned north on the intersection up ahead, we'd cross the Montlake Bridge, a drawbridge that allowed ships passage through the Cut and which connected the north shore with the south shore.

I rather doubted we would cross, however; the north shore was dedicated mostly to the University of Washington. Sure enough, we intersected Montlake Boulevard and continued west on East Shelby. The houses were graceful but aging, lawns well-kept but not obsessively so. It was exactly the kind of neighborhood where Ian would live—not slummy or urban but not pretentious either, because he was none of those things.

We walked side by side, Russ and I, our strides steadily eating up the distance between the terror of not knowing and a grief so deep I could barely fathom it. But I've never been a coward, and I didn't falter. Just as I had once been forced to confess to Zanna that I had committed the most heinous of the Best Friend's Unpardonable Sins, I didn't shrink from facing what was waiting for me in Ian's house.

As we approached a curve in the road where East Shelby Street became West Park Drive East, Russ paused, turning toward a large Victorian on our right. It was obvious the owner was in the middle of painting it; large splotches of flaking paint had been scraped away, and a ladder lay along the side of the house. The trim was already neatly smoothed and freshly coated with rich color.

"Are you ready, Suzanne?"

I swallowed over a hard lump in my throat. "What are we going to find inside?"

"I don't know," he admitted. "I didn't scout ahead. I didn't want to leave you when you were so distraught."

"Is this really his house?"

Russ sniffed the air, inhaling deeply, eyes closed, and he nodded. "Yes."

I stared at the house, trying to envision Ian painting the lap siding sage green, applying the terra cotta red to the eaves, a lighter terra cotta orange to the trim around the windows. I could see his fetish for detail encouraging him to brush burnt yellow in accent X's above the windows and in various other small areas that made the whole color scheme pop.

It didn't take much imagination. Ian was very creative, and earth tones were his bag. I could see him on a cool spring day, his wide-shouldered, muscled frame encased in an earth-brown pull-over sweater, raking a hand through his windblown hair as he matched exterior paint chips to find the best combination of colors for the Queen Anne Victorian before us now.

I felt drawn to the house, pulled toward it as though coming home. The colors beckoned me, spoke of comfort and acceptance, rest and peace. I knew then that Russ was right: this was Ian's house, and he had painted it all the colors I loved best, all the colors that had pervaded our cozy apartment.

He had painted this house for me.

My feet stopped. I was unable to make them take another step, although walking was a relief compared to the ache from ankle to hip when standing still. Russ stopped beside me and simply waited.

"It's my house," I whispered. "He did it for me."

"Yes," he whispered back.

"Why?" I was only vaguely aware of the tears pouring down my cheeks. "Why would he do that?"

"He knew Raum had left you. He always knew that someday you'd come up this walk."

"That's silly." But even if it was silly, it was also sweet. Sweet and sad and futile, because, as with Zanna, I'd come too damn late.

"That's faith," Russ corrected softly. "What are you afraid of? Why did you stop?"

I couldn't drag my eyes from the house. "You know why."

"Say it and face it, Suzanne."

42

"I'm afraid I'm too late. That he's . . . that he's . . ."

"Dead?"

"Yes."

He inhaled long and deep of the afternoon air, scenting something on the mild breeze blowing across the Montlake Cut, but he didn't tell me what. The day had taken on the golden light of a summer afternoon, that ageless quality when you're certain that time has stopped and you can live an eternity without aging, drinking your fill of life and love and youth until your soul is drunk with it.

It came to me suddenly in that still, timeless moment what had bothered me earlier when I'd been thinking of Raum.

Can't you just . . . fly us somewhere?

He lied to you about that. It doesn't work that way.

"Russ," I said slowly, still staring out at the Cut. "Do you know how I met Raum?"

"He was wounded and you found him, nursed him back to health." He shrugged, unconcerned.

"He crash-landed on the roof of my apartment. We—Ian and I—lived in one of those classy old brick apartment buildings with a flat roof that was set up as a courtyard, with raised gardens and those quaint little wrought iron ice cream tables."

He didn't say anything, just waited for me to continue, one brow raised over a copper-colored eye.

"I was on the roof at one in the morning, drinking wine and thinking about Zanna. It was her birthday."

My eyes didn't see the Painted Lady before me now; they looked into the past to the hot summer night that had changed my life. I don't know if I'd heard a sound or seen a shadow, but something had made me look up in time to see the angel descending from the sky like judgment itself, glorious wings unfurled, black against the midnight-blue sky. Black to match his hair.

He saw me looking up. Perhaps I'd made a sound to alert

him. He checked his flight in alarm, caught his foot on the roof of the enclosed stairway, and crashed onto the gravel with a shout of pain.

Then his eyes caught mine, green like a verdant meadow, a green unlike anything on this earth, and that was the start of the unraveling of my will.

"He should have been invisible. He never should have taken the chance and allowed you to see him."

"I know. He told me. But I did see him, and from the first look it was too late. He'd fallen on his wing and sprained it, so he couldn't shift his appearance completely, just enough to make his wings mostly unnoticeable under a tee-shirt. He couldn't fly, either. So I took him downstairs to our apartment, gave him a shirt and a cover story, and woke Ian."

And that was the beginning of our end. Ian became insubstantial when compared to the angel, and even though Raum had tried to fade into the background, in a small amount of time he completely eclipsed my human lover. I had let Ian go with hardly a qualm and had not regretted it once until after Raum had left me and I'd come back to my human senses.

"But you didn't get the point of this story, Russ. He had wings. He was flying. You told me angels don't fly."

He looked stunned. "When did I ever tell you that?"

"When I first met you. I asked if you could just fly us to wherever we were going, and you said he lied to me about that, it didn't work that way."

He stared at me openmouthed, and then began laughing. He laughed long and hard before he brought himself under control and slipped his arm around me.

"Forgive me, Suzanne. That struck me as very funny."

"I'm glad you think so."

"It's just that you humans are so literal." He turned me around to face him, and cupped his hands on either side of my face. "I didn't mean we can't fly. I meant that we can't just fly you to wherever we need you to go. We're a marvel of balance and strength. Our wingspan and the strength of the muscles required to fly are enough to serve us . . . but not enough to carry a passenger."

Hot color flooded my face and I tried to turn away. "Oh." I frowned again.

"What else?"

"You said you can't vanish from here and appear in Venice in an instant. Is that true?"

He sighed. "Your instant or my instant?"

"Is there a difference?"

"Major difference. A year in your realm is just a blip in time for me."

"So what looks like an instantaneous jump from one continent to another to me actually takes less time," I pointed out.

"No. We don't . . . it doesn't work that way." He waved a hand impatiently, frustrated at my lack of comprehension. "It's so hard to explain to a human. When we move long distances, we don't move in this realm. It's easier for us in our own dimension. Time is different for us there, more like time is here for you. By your standards, we relocate instantaneously, but moving through my realm is to me like taking a long journey."

"Then why not travel through mine?"

"We can't fly across the ocean without a rest."

"Can't you just land in the water and rest?"

He quirked a wry smile at me. "Sure, if I want to drown. I can die just like you can, Suzanne. I have to swim to stay afloat. And then my wings get wet, and they have to dry before I can fly again." He shook his head. "Your species has some odd ideas about angels."

I studied him with suspicion for another long moment, but he didn't flinch away from my gaze, and I finally decided he was telling the truth. I let a smile curve my mouth just a little.

"All right. I'm sorry. I didn't mean to sound like I don't trust you."

"You *shouldn't* trust me, Suzanne," he countered harshly. "I said I'm able to resist the temptation of your species, but I never said I was immune to your attraction. You're right to question me, to reserve your trust. You've already been ill-used by my kind."

"But you're helping me track him down and bring him to justice."

"That doesn't make me a paragon of virtue. I'm just as susceptible to temptation as the next angel."

"Well, that doesn't exactly put me at ease."

"Good. Now shall we go?"

I turned my attention back to the house. Again the color palette called to me, beckoning me, seducing me. A house painted just for me, by a man who had every reason to hate me but, from all evidence, had not.

"Yes, let's go."

The walk was long and winding, carrying us past tasteful gardens. Flowers bloomed riotously, thriving in the capricious Seattle weather. The lawn was lush and freshly mown; the sweet scent of newly cut grass still lingered in the warm air.

The flagstone walk ended, and now I could see the tools of Ian's labor on the front porch: paint cans, long wooden stir sticks, rags, rollers, brushes, rolls of plastic sheeting. And—so Ian that I nearly fell to my knees and wept—the brown pull-over sweater I'd envisioned him wearing, tossed carelessly over the back of a wooden Adirondack stained the same orange terra cotta as the trim around the windows.

My knees trembled as we went up the steps. My whole body shook by the time we crossed the wide planks of the porch. I thought I might faint as Russ raised his hand and rapped on the screen door, and then opened it and turned the front door knob, letting us into the foyer.

Ian's voice rang out from the back of the house—"Be there in a minute!"—for he hadn't heard our silent entry.

He was alive!

Russ fell in behind me as I tracked Ian's voice down the

narrow hallway. His back was to us as we entered the kitchen, a snug tee-shirt flexed over his muscular shoulders as he cut oranges into wedges. My eyes drank him in, my heart swelling with relief, but I could take no more steps. A gulf remained between us, broader than the ten feet that separated us. It was the gulf of betrayal and pain and abandonment.

The years had been kind to him, at least from what I could see. He was still trim and straight-bodied, well-muscled, and silver had yet to thread its way through his hair.

Ian turned. His eyes behind the familiar gold-rimmed glasses opened wide with shock. The bowl of orange wedges slipped from his paint-speckled hands and shattered on the floor.

"Suzanne!" Barely a whisper, his voice cracked, broke. "Oh my God, Suzanne!"

Shock rooted me to the floor, mingled with a wild hope that my journey had come to an end. "You can see me? Please, Ian, tell me you can really see me!"

"Of course I can I see you, but..." He broke off and rushed toward me, glass crunching under his sneakers. His hands closed on my shoulders, frantically clenching and releasing, clenching and releasing, reassuring himself that I was real.

Relief crashed through me like a flash flood through a dry canyon. I hadn't disappeared, and I wasn't a ghost. Russ had brought me through, a little worse for wear, maybe, but alive and delivered into the hands of safety.

Bewilderment creased Ian's brow, and his hands settled, gripping my upper arms. "Where have you *been*, Suzanne? I've been frantic!"

A cold chill raced down my spine. "What are you talking about?"

He took three steps to the right, snagged a newspaper from a careless stack on the breakfast table, and shoved it in my face. The same paper I'd seen at Zanna's, dated two days ago, but this time I could read the whole headline.

Police call off search for missing bank executive Suzanne Harper after six weeks.

Chapter Six

My legs collapsed under me. Ian lunged forward, barely catching me before I fell. My weight bore us clumsily to the floor, his body cushioning mine as I crumpled like an accordion.

"You're so thin," he whispered, and then he began to cry. No great, whooping sobs for Ian—oh no, that would never do. He cried quietly, tears flooding from his eyes and down his cheeks in a silent stream. He pressed his face against my neck and held me with all the desperation of a drowning man.

I was so tired I could make no sense of the headline he'd shown me. *Missing for six weeks.* That had to be a mistake; Russ had come to me outside the deli in Queen Anne only three days ago. But hadn't I thought, not so long ago, that I was missing large stretches of time? Could that have been an accurate assessment?

Russ. Damn that son-of-a-bitch—he had taken me through his realm on our travels! I couldn't believe it; what if he'd not been paying attention and had let me spend too much time in his world? Years could have passed—decades, even—by the time we'd ventured back into the human dimension. I could have died from malnourishment and thirst. I couldn't believe he'd taken such a risk without asking permission.

I looked up to berate him, but he had retreated out of sight, allowing my reunion with Ian to remain private and unimpeded by his presence—and awkward explanations.

It didn't matter right now what Russ had done to keep

me safe on this dark journey. What mattered was Ian's arms around me, Ian's scent filling my nose, the comforting thud of Ian's heart against my side. I'd forgotten, in the years he'd been gone, how much the steady beat of that human organ meant to me. I sagged into his embrace, leaned my head against the cabinet behind us, and slept.

* * *

I woke to birds chirping outside the bedroom window and the glorious sensation of having spent an indecent number of hours in blissful, dreamless slumber. I rolled over, my aching body delighting in the cushion of a real bed, and found Ian sprawled beside me on top of the covers. He'd slept in his clothes, but they were different clothes than he'd been wearing when I'd arrived.

I tugged my pillow into a more comfortable position and caught a whiff of shampoo. Fragments of yesterday—was it yesterday?—swirled in my memory: a much-needed shower; a change of clothes (nothing fancier than one of Ian's tee-shirts and a pair of sweat shorts cinched in at the waist so they billowed around my hips like clown pants); a bowl of oatmeal—suitably bland for one who'd not had a real meal in days (*weeks*—had it really been *weeks*?)—and a couple wedges of wheat toast.

Then Ian had bundled me onto the sofa, but how I had made it to his bedroom upstairs was anyone's guess. More missing pieces of time. I was starting to think my days spent with Russ had left Swiss cheese holes in my memory.

Ian's face bore its own marks from my ordeal. Sleepless nights had left discolored shadows under his eyes, and stress had carved deep lines around his eyes and mouth. An unruly lock of hair lay over his forehead, touching his lashes and making him frown in his sleep. I reached out and brushed it away. His forehead was creased even in slumber, as though he worried while unconscious.

My heart broke at that thought. I stroked his face, smoothing away the lines, and he stirred, his eyes opening. Relief skimmed across his face, and I wondered what he'd been dreaming. The misery I'd put this man through since the day I'd met him... It was a wonder he hadn't thrown me out of his house.

But he smiled as he murmured, "Hey, Suze."

"Ian." I smiled back, my face crumpling almost instantly. His smile turned to alarm.

"Hey, hey!"

He scooted over, and for the next thirty seconds embarked on an almost comical attempt to reach me through the blankets on top of me. But in the end he found me and pulled me close, smoothing his hand over my hair, which rioted all over my head because it had been wet when I'd gone to sleep.

"None of that now. You're all right now. It's all right."

"I don't understand any of this. I've only been gone three days, Ian. Why would everyone think I've been gone six weeks?"

He stared at me in disbelief. "What day do you think it is?"

"July ninth. Or maybe, at most, the tenth. I met Russ at . . . the . . . "

Where *was* Russ? I remembered him falling into step behind me as we walked through Ian's house to the kitchen and looking for him as I huddled, exhausted, on Ian's kitchen floor. I knew angels could hide their presence from humans, but it was strange that he would have just left me here—unless he had found Raum, and thought I was safer left in Ian's care while he dealt with the rogue angel.

"Who is Russ?" Ian asked, the edge in his voice so slight I might have imagined it.

I pushed a hand through my hair, unknotting some of the tangles. "There's so much I have to tell you, and I don't know where to start. I don't even think you'll believe most of it."

"Suzanne . . . it's August twelfth," Ian said gently. "You've lost five and a half weeks of time. Where have you been? And *who* is Russ?"

"Icarus," I replied vacantly. "He flew too close to the sun."

He looked truly alarmed now. "Did you hit your head? Or did you have a nervous breakdown? I know . . . I heard that Raum left you." *Three years ago. Three years ago and you're only now coming to me.* Those were the words he wanted to say. I could hear them as clearly as though he'd actually said them.

I looked at him, my tears blurring his face so that I couldn't gauge his expression. "I—I didn't know how."

"How what?"

"How to find my way back."

"Back where, Suze?" His voice was gentle, but his expression—clear now because the tears had spilled from my eyes and were running down my face—was petrified.

"To my life. Life before the *malakhim*. Will you listen without interrupting? Let me tell you everything, then if you'll feed me and give me bus fare, I'll go home and you won't have to see me again."

He floundered for a reply, his mouth working words that his tongue couldn't force out. Eventually, he fell back on his I-must-be-gentle-and-placate-the-crazy-woman tone.

"It doesn't work that way, honey. The police have been looking for you for weeks—you simply vanished off the street, Suzanne! Your car was found parked outside a café in Queen Anne, but the waitress can't remember you being there. Your coworkers are beside themselves—the bank is offering a reward for information on your whereabouts. You can't just waltz back in like you missed one day of work and forgot to call in sick!"

He'd said too many words for me to process, so I simply disregarded them and went on like he hadn't spoken. "He came out of nowhere while I was walking to my car and asked to talk to me. I knew what he was right away, and why he was there. He was looking for Raum, because of what Raum . . . because of what he's become."

"You're making no sense."

"He's an angel." His mouth tightened. "A real angel, Ian, as in not human. From another realm. Wings and all."

I didn't imagine him pulling slightly away from me.

"Suzanne, that's . . . that's crazy."

"I know."

But crazy or not, I continued with my story, telling him everything I could remember about the time I'd spent walking Seattle with Russ, tracking Raum. About the two years I'd spent with Raum, and the three years in desperate limbo after he left me. About the murders. What little color was left in his face abruptly drained when I told him of being at Zanna's house and finding his ring in the lawn.

"I lost it at Zanna's house. One second it was on my finger; the next, gone without a trace. The crime lab people looked for it but never found it."

"Were you there often?"

Ian sensed what I was really asking. "That was the first time I'd been there. She still had us both listed as emergency contacts. But you were missing, so they called me."

I simply nodded. It didn't really surprise me. Zanna had always been a very constant little thing. "When I came yesterday, I—"

Ian broke in again. "Suzanne, you got here two days ago. You've spent most of it sleeping—all of it, actually, since you came home from the hospital."

"Hospital!" I exclaimed. "I don't remember going to the hospital."

The lines of worry deepened around his eyes and mouth. "What did you think I would do when you showed up in this kind of condition? I took you to the hospital. They hooked you to an IV to hydrate you, bandaged up your feet, and kept you overnight for observation."

I stared at him, deeply afraid now. I had no memory of the events he was describing.

"Do you remember talking to the police?" he asked, and then shook his head. "No, of course you wouldn't, not if you don't even remember being at the hospital. They took your statement."

"I was able to give one?"

"Perfectly lucid, but there was none of this . . . this . . . malamute crap."

"*Malakhim*," I corrected absently.

"Whatever. You told them you had no idea where you'd been, you had no memory of anything after leaving work the day you disappeared. Suze—" He bit his lip, and then plunged on. "They even did a rape kit and took your clothes for evidence."

"I wasn't raped," I said sharply, and then, uncertainly, "Was I?"

"They don't think so." He placed a slight emphasis on the word *think*. "But you *were* dehydrated and malnourished and on the brink of exhaustion. The hospital wanted to keep you longer, but I assured them I could take care of you just as well, so they released you into my care." He sounded as though he doubted the wisdom of that action now.

"And the police—what are they doing? I wasn't kidnapped, Ian; I went with Russ willingly. Raum has to be found and stopped, but the authorities can't help with that. If the *malakhim* don't want to be seen by humans, they won't be."

He drew in a sharp breath through his nostrils, signaling his struggle for patience. "Which is why I have yet to see this Russ fellow?"

"Yes."

"How very convenient, Suzanne. I can't say you're lying to me—I have no evidence that you're not telling the truth because this guy can turn invisible."

Oh, I had been wrong—Ian wasn't struggling for patience

but for belief.

"Ian."

"I suffered through Raum. I did what you asked me to do, and I left. I waited for you to come to your senses. And three years—*three years* —after he left you, you finally come to me. And what do I hear?"

"Ian, why would I lie about this? Think about it."

"Some cock-and-bull story about angels. This is one story I don't think I can swallow."

"Then perhaps I should leave," I said quietly. "Because if you haven't believed me yet, you're never going to. I didn't have a chance once Raum came into my life. You can believe that or not. And when he left . . . I couldn't find my own way out of the mess; how could I expect to involve you in it?"

Ian opened his mouth to speak, but I went on before he could make some stupid man remark and piss me off.

"Do you know what I expected to find here, Ian? I expected to find you dead. When I found your ring at Zanna's—when I saw the lopsided heart and realized it was yours—I thought my heart had died right in my chest.

"I remember screaming. That's all I remember until I woke up in a park down at the end of this street, wanting to die, too. I don't know how many days it's been since I found the ring . . . I think maybe Russ has been taking me through his realm sometimes to cut the distance we've had to travel while we've been tracking Raum. Time is different in their realm."

Ian's eyes took up most of his face. My matter-of-fact, practical tone scared him more than anything else. Had I come in raving and shrieking and flinching at sudden movements or unexpected sounds, he probably would have handled it better. He'd have lain back down beside me, forced a sleeping pill into me, and set his mind to the problem of how to fix me.

But how do you fix crazy when it doesn't know it's

crazy? I could see the question circling in his mind, showing plainly in his eyes as apprehension.

"I have proof," I said suddenly, struggling to pull the neck of the tee-shirt down to show him the marks of the *malakhim* bonds.

"I've seen," he said shortly. "I'd like to get my hands around the throat of the person who did it. And where is the ring now, by the way? You came here with nothing but the clothes on your back. No jewelry at all. Why are you making up this elaborate story to explain why you disappeared?"

I stared at him in silence, and then pushed the covers off me, swinging my legs out of bed.

"Oh, come on, Suzanne," he groaned, collapsing backward onto his pillows. "You always do this when you get angry with me."

"Do what, exactly?"

"Run away."

"I'm not running. I'm going home. There's no reason for me to stay here if you don't believe me. I can take care of myself."

"Oh, *that's* obvious." His derisive snort incensed me more than anything else, but before I could respond, he said, "You can't leave. The police are supposed to come by later this afternoon with some follow-up questions. I assured them you would be here under my watchful eye."

"You're treating me like I'm some sort of criminal, Ian," I said sharply. "That's very insulting."

"I'm treating you like a traumatized woman who has been missing for six weeks," he countered in a level voice. "And I'm not about to let some crazy kidnapping asshole have another whack at you."

A movement in the doorway caught my eye. Russ was leaning against the doorjamb, quite entertained by our conversation.

"Russ," I said.

"Him again," Ian muttered violently. "What about him?"

I started to point at the doorway, but Russ shook his head

and put a finger to his lips. My hand went up to rake through my tangled hair instead.

"I was just calling him to see if he would deign to make an appearance. A little proof to substantiate my story would be nice."

Russ didn't miss the bite in my voice. His grin widened. He beckoned to me to follow him, and I wondered just how I was going to escape Ian's watchful eye.

"I have to use the bathroom." I slid off the bed, wincing as my wounded feet took my weight, and headed toward the door.

"The bathroom's through there," Ian said, pointing at a door on the opposite side of the room. That figured—access from the bedroom. I pretended not to hear, and his exasperated sigh followed me as I bounced off the door jamb and limped into the hallway.

"What do you want?" I hissed as soon as I estimated we were out of Ian's earshot.

"I want to show you something. Come on—er—can you walk?" he asked skeptically, eyeing my old-woman hobble with doubt. "I think you were faring better in my care."

"You're the only one who thinks so," I muttered. "I have some questions for you, such as why can Ian see me? I thought I was shielded."

"You *were* shielded. I lifted it in the park before we came here."

"Why? And how? I don't remember you doing anything special."

"Doesn't take a circle of thirteen, incantations, and a blood sacrifice," he said, chuckling. "I simply ran my hand down your back. Shielding gone. Presto chango."

I rolled my eyes. "You're no magician."

"No," he agreed. "I'm much, much more."

"Why did you leave me here? Why didn't you say anything to Ian? You know he doesn't believe anything I've told him."

"Then why did you tell him? Personally I would have kept it to myself. I thought you would be safer with him than with me from here on out."

I stopped, leaning against the hallway wall. Russ kept walking, his hand outstretched to open a door directly in front of us where the hall ended.

"You found Raum."

"Yes. But first I want to show you something. Can you walk a little farther?"

"I think so." I grimaced as I took another couple of steps.

"Come on, then." He opened the door before him, and waited for me to precede him up what appeared to be the steps to the attic. "If you fall, fall backward. I'll catch you."

"Likely story," I muttered, and he chuckled again.

Halfway up the steps, I muttered "The attic, Russ? How am I going to explain this?"

"He already thinks you're crazy, so what's it matter?"

"Good point."

I stepped up, flinching, and grabbed the handrail to haul myself onto the next step. My feet were in raw, blistered agony, which reminded me...

"You took me through your realm, didn't you? I haven't been gone only three days. I really have been gone six weeks."

"There was no other way, Suzanne. I had to work around your human limitations."

"I don't remember hardly anything about the last month, Russ. You realize that, don't you?"

"That happens when a human goes through our realm: you sleep, or something close to it. Your physicians call it being comatose or catatonic. It's rare for one to remember anything of the journey. It was the best I could do at the time. Maybe not the wisest choice, I admit."

He quirked a brow at me as I glared over my shoulder at him.

"Did you need those six weeks, Suzanne? Would you have done anything other than wallow in the misery of Raum

58

having left you and knowing what he's become?"

I paused, leaning against the wall and shifting from foot to foot to relieve the agony. "No, probably not."

Three steps to go. My feet screamed at the thought. Two steps. The dull throb from heel to thigh blossomed into full-fledged pain. One step. My legs trembled, and I hoped there was a chair to sit in when we got up there. Walking had been a bad idea.

At last, I reached the top and took a couple more shuffling steps to allow room for Russ to come in behind me. The attic was surprisingly well lit; a floor-to-ceiling arched window with panes of leaded glass let in daylight. I could see sailboats on the Montlake Cut, canvas rippling in the breeze, looking impossibly tiny from this distance and height.

"So why are we up here?"

The room was utterly empty except for a chair across the room and a neat cluster of construction tools and supplies; obviously Ian was working on this area of the house.

"To give him the proof he needs," Russ replied easily.

I turned to give him a questioning look and saw Ian hovering on the steps behind us, his face anxious and wary. Russ flicked a hand, and the door at the bottom of the stairs slammed shut. Ian jumped, whirling around, and when he turned back, his expression was fearful.

"Suze—"

"Shh," Russ said gently, and the rest of Ian's words dried up as his vocal cords seized. Panic clawed its way onto his face.

"Stop it, Russ. This isn't funny. This isn't how I want to prove to him that I'm telling the truth."

His eyes turned my way, and I stepped back, my brain spinning in freefall. No longer were they any of the colors he'd affected through our short acquaintance, but instead all colors and no color, a swirling kaleidoscope of every hue in the universe. His human façade shimmered like heat waves on hot tarmac, and then he was all angel: humanoid body, russet wings, a face that transcended beauty and stole both breath and rational thought. He was made of light that had mass, substance. I stared, transfixed.

"You want him to know the truth. Here is the truth."

His hand shot out, and my heart leapt into my throat. But he only swept his fingertips over Ian's eyes and lips. Ian blinked once, twice, and then his eyes focused on Russ. Widened until his eyeballs were in danger of falling from their sockets. Wonder battled fear, each claiming victories only to fall in the next second to the other.

"Oh. My. God." said Ian, slowly and deliberately.

"Hardly." Russ laughed a little.

Ian's eyes traveled from Russ to the chair across the room, and his face went impossibly white. He opened his mouth, but Russ said "Shh, Ian." Ian's mouth closed with an audible snap as he was struck mute again.

Russ reached casually toward me. My gaze fastened on the chair, anxious for illumination, as I let him brush his fingertips over my eyes as he had Ian's.

My legs trembled, collapsed. A fine tremor raced through my body, intensifying until I shook like a sapling in a high wind. Raum sat in the chair, bound securely to its frame and gagged so tightly no sound would be able to escape no matter how hard he tried. But his eyes spoke when his mouth could not, and they caught and held mine in a steady gaze, beseeching, apologetic. Regretful.

With no warning, Ian was launched toward the arched window by an invisible force. I shrieked in horror as he crashed through the glass and into the warm August air, his scream of terror silent, his arms windmilling, seeking purchase. At the last possible second, his scrabbling fingers found the sill, and the wall shook with the impact of his body as it swung against the house. Blood ran in rivulets from the window sill as shards of thick glass punctured his flesh.

For one second that lasted an eternity, I huddled on the floor, utterly paralyzed with shock, caught in a triangle of confusion and conflicting loyalties. On one side, my human lover, who clung with bloody fingers to precarious safety; on another, my angelic lover, bound and gagged and probably a vicious, conscienceless killer; and on the third side an avenging angel glowering over the scene, magnificent in his righteous fury, a tower of blinding light and heavenly justice.

I forced myself to stand, my trembling legs barely able to hold me up. Raum's eyes never left mine. Russ's eyes never left Raum. In the brief space of time it took for my heart to beat once, my eyes catalogued every detail in the deafeningly silent room. Only one stood out with painful clarity: Ian's hands, slick with blood, had begun to slip from the window sill.

Chapter Seven

I lunged for the window. The air turned to sludge, slowing my leap to an awkward lurch. Or maybe it was just my panic making me torpid and clumsy. My fingers scrabbled over the back of Ian's left hand as it lost its grip and flailed out into space. Sunlight glinted off the jagged shards of glass embedded in his palm.

His right hand was slipping, his fingers slick with an amazing amount of blood. I slammed my hand down on it to hold it on the sill, and he screamed silently as glass sank deeper into his flesh. My other hand seized his shirt, but in my weakened state I was only prolonging the inevitable.

"Please. *Please.*" I don't know to whom I was pleading: perhaps Raum, whom I suspected had thrown Ian out the window. Or maybe Russ, whom stood frozen in place, unable to look away from Raum. Or perhaps God, whom I felt had let me suffer enough trials and heartbreak over the last five years.

I threw a desperate look over my shoulder at Russ, tears of fear and horror spilling down my cheeks. *"Help me, dammit!"*

Russ's head turned toward me, agonizingly slow. Ian's shirt slipped from my fingers and I heaved myself farther out the window, grabbing hold of a belt loop and praying the factory hadn't skimped on quality when making his jeans. I felt myself slipping over the sill, Ian's weight dragging me over the edge.

And then Russ was there, pulling us both back inside with a mighty heave. He left us huddled beneath the broken window, shaken and bleeding, and resumed his silent vigil near the door.

"Are you all right, Suzanne?" he asked in a remote, courteous voice. "Ian?"

"F-fine," I stammered, and began to shake. Ian looked afraid to move; his eyes were wide and staring, reliving his horrifying flight into thin air on the film screen of his mind. His face was so white I feared he might be bleeding out. But I didn't think there were any arteries in one's palms, and he didn't look like he'd been hurt anywhere else.

"Russ . . ." I hesitated. He turned toward me, and I was heartened by his acknowledgment. "Why is Raum here? Why is he tied up in Ian's attic?"

"I wanted you to witness justice, Suzanne," he said, his voice strange. "Don't you want justice?"

My gaze swung between the two *malakhim*, from Russ's burning, timeless eyes to Raum's gaze, steady and calm but still full of that terrible regret.

Something wasn't right.

"Russ," I said cautiously. "Take off Raum's gag. I want to hear it from his lips."

He cocked his head to one side. "Hear what?"

"His confession."

"It's not a good idea, Suzanne. He'll try to persuade you, seduce you with what you want to hear. As your protector, I can't—"

"Take it off."

His kaleidoscope eyes stared at me, unnerving in their unwavering scrutiny. Without pupils and depthless, they were windows into heaven itself.

He turned away without answering, and crossed the room in three long strides. It *looked* like he untied the gag, but it simply swirled away like dissipating light and vanished. Beside me, Ian began hyperventilating.

"Ease up on Ian. Give him back his voice."

Russ shook his head. "He'll scream. He's losing it." He

nodded toward Ian, and I stole a glance at him, not daring to take my eyes from Russ for more than a split second for fear he would kill Raum out of hand and I would never hear his explanations.

He was right—Ian *was* losing it. His whole body shook and his breath came in short gasps. His eyes crept to the two *malakhim* across the room, and I could see the scream rising in him, could read it in his eyes.

I silently conceded the point to Russ and turned to look at Raum, who was flexing his jaw in relief. Still, his eyes never left my face, not even to check the location of his captor and soon-to-be executioner.

I pushed to my feet, gently dislodging Ian's panicked grip. My legs trembled badly as I crossed the room. My body flushed hot and cold and hot again. Fear fluttered through me, making my muscles weak and shaky. I stopped two feet away from Raum, ignoring Russ as he shifted closer to me. I looked down into Raum's eyes. Like Russ's they had no pupils, no irises. They shone like flawless gems, with mists of color scudding across their surface. Eyes of eternity. Eyes of another world.

The eyes of a traitorous lover, of a fallen Son of God.

"Did you do it?" I whispered.

Flares of glorious light flashed in his eyes. "Run, Suzanne," he whispered back.

My hand clapped over my mouth, stifling a sob. Disappointment and betrayal ran deep, like a sword through my soul. He couldn't mean it. I didn't want to believe it. I had so adamantly resisted believing Russ that I had forgotten my own suspicions, pushed them aside in my desire to be reunited with him.

"Run," he repeated. "Now."

Eyes flashing like sheet lightning, he broke his bonds with a roar of rage and launched himself out of the chair.

I stumbled backward, my response to his warning coming too late to get out of the way. His shoulder hit me low in the abdomen and knocked me flying into Russ, who shunted me aside as easily as he would a bothersome newspaper in a windstorm. I hit the floor with bruising force, the wind knocked from me. He met Raum in mid-air, their bodies crashing together in a soundless symphony of motion and exploding light.

Raum's lip curled back in a snarl that erupted into a full-fledged howl of rage. Ian cowered against the wall, his arms covering his head. I cringed as the howl wavered to a deafening crescendo above the thundering heartbeat in my ears. Splintering pain shot through my arm as tried to use it to lever myself upright. Broken.

The angels hit the floor with a tremendous crash. I couldn't tell who had thrown whom, but their savage battle rolled them close to Ian and me. With Russ's arm across his throat, Raum managed to raise his head, his wild eyes unerringly fixing on me.

"Run!" he rasped. "Take Ian and run! I can only hold him off for a few minutes. *Now, Suza—*"

Russ tightened his grip, cutting off Raum's voice. Fury broke across Raum's face, and he twisted out of Russ's hold. The battle raged across the room, leaving us a clear path to the door.

I crawled to Ian's side, holding my broken arm as close to my body as I could to keep it still and protected. "Ian, come on. *Come on!*"

Poking and prodding, hectoring and nagging, I herded him toward the steps like a demented sheep dog. He staggered down the steps, losing his balance and skidding down four before landing on his backside. His hands came up to break his fall and left bloody smears along the wall, the railing, and the wooden treads. I crouched beside him, trying to lever him up with my good arm. His eyes bulged in their sockets, the brain behind them frantically trying to come to grips with what he'd seen and experienced. I wrenched open the door just as the sound floated up from the main floor, melodic and incongruous to the battle that rampaged through the attic. The doorbell.

The police are supposed to come by later this afternoon with some follow-up questions. I assured them you would be here under my watchful eye.

A glance at Ian's eyes told me the police would be convinced they'd left me in the care of a mad crack addict.

With violent force, the door wrenched out of my hand and slammed closed, nearly dislocating my shoulder and shutting Ian and me in the attic. I twisted the knob and yanked, screaming with rage, but the door had sealed itself shut.

Ian slumped into the corner, curling into a ball, hiding his face against his thighs. He was thoroughly in denial. I felt more than a trace of anger and irritation; why did I have to be the one to face this? Why couldn't he stand beside me, support me, partners against fear and angelic rage?

The anger vanished in the next instant. I'd had plenty of time—years—to come to terms with the existence and nature of angels. Ian's ordered beliefs had been shaken to their very foundation.

I crept back up the stairs, cradling my arm, and peered around the corner in time to see Russ drive what looked like a flaming fist toward Raum's face at impossible speed. At the last second, Raum ducked, and the wall behind him exploded, raining fragments of drywall across the attic floor.

I saw it lying on the floor at the edge of the battle: a sword made of flaming light so white it looked blue, and understood then what I'd seen. Not a fist of fire, but a blade of prismatic light. Russ was distracted trying to slice Raum out of existence. Raum had his hands full fending him off, ducking and dodging because he'd lost his blade in the battle.

I was pretty certain neither would notice if I crept up

and snatched Raum's sword. I started forward.

Raum's eyes locked on mine like a homing beacon. I froze. Russ, noticing Raum's distraction, started to turn toward me but Raum, flicking a glance at me and then at the sword, engaged him in battle again, coming on with such violence that Russ was hard-pressed to defend himself.

I remained frozen in place for several long seconds. Raum wanted me to get the sword; he'd deliberately distracted Russ so that I could sneak in and make the grab. Had he deliberately lost it, too? But why would he want me to have the weapon? He was a cold-blooded killer . . . wasn't he?

I drew in a breath, narrowed my gaze so that I saw only the sword, and sprinted forward. I was grace personified, the very definition of speed. I was a lithe whirlwind, fleet of foot and quick of hand. I danced through the battle as it raged back and forth over the sword, dodging, lunging, reaching, grasping—

In reality, I staggered into the middle of the fray, my equilibrium erased by my ordeal and their deafening combat, tripped over Raum's leg, and sprawled in an untidy heap at the edge of the conflict. By some miracle, my hand clutched the sword when I lurched to my feet.

I spun away from the warring *malakhim* in a mad pirouette and raised the sword. It rang like the finest crystal, as though I'd pulled it from a gemstone sheath. Both angels froze, the battle forgotten. Shock scuttled across Russ's face. Raum smiled with vulpine triumph.

The blade weighed nothing, as though I held a spear of light. Pain vanished, and I knew no worries. No fear. No pain. The flaming light of the sword engulfed me, singing through my nerve endings, and I knew in that moment that I stood in the very presence of God.

"Let him go," I said to Russ. My voice rang with authority, and a small part of me still felt human enough to be stunned when he immediately obeyed. "Let him speak."

Raum rubbed his throat, sending a smoking glare at Russ before turning his full attention on me. "I am sorry, Suzanne."

"Did you do it?"

He drew in a steadying breath. "If you mean the murders," he said evenly, "No. I did not."

"Who did?"

Without expression, he directed his gaze at Russ. "Your 'friend' Icarus would be the guilty party."

Russ's mouth twisted into a sneer. "*Would* be? Only if you can manage to frame me for it. Don't believe him, Suzanne. You've spent six weeks with me. If I were a murderer, wouldn't I have killed you by now? I've had plenty of opportunity."

Raum ignored him. "He captured me shortly after I left you. I'd been sent to protect you because he had set his sights on you. You weren't supposed to see me." If he'd had a heart, I swear I would have seen it breaking in his eyes.

"But you did. And I couldn't help it. I'd never had to interact with you before; I'd been there to protect you, silent, invisible. But once you saw me, once I knew you . . . oh, Suzanne, forgive me. I had no right to love you, to ruin your love for Ian. Forgive me."

Laughter rang through the room, and behind it I could hear the thud of running footsteps coming up the stairs to the second floor. The police had broken in. Russ, still laughing, didn't appear concerned.

"Oh, that's rich. You were sent to protect her, and you seduced her instead? You were sent to protect her, but you left her without a thought to that protection? Your track record speaks for itself." He turned to me, morphing his shape into the human guise with which I was so familiar, his eyes turning the copper color he somehow knew I favored.

"Don't be fooled by your human emotions, Suzanne. He left you, period. He cared so little for you that he simply walked away, leaving you marked and scarred and utterly alone. I've shielded you, cared for you, stayed by your side, fed you, clothed you, carried you—"

Raum snorted. "He sounds like he's campaigning to be the Christ. Think about it, Suzanne. How many newspapers have you seen since you met him? How much television? You didn't even know you'd been with him for six weeks, did you? And look at you—you call that care? You're malnourished, dehydrated, weak, and traumatized.

"I left you, but I didn't *leave*. I was there, watching over you, until this jackass got the jump on me and hijacked me. I've been bound up in this attic for two and a half human years, unable to break the bonds, while he laid his plans and left his trail of bodies."

A heavy hand hammered at the attic door. "Police! Open the door NOW!"

Raum paid it no attention, but Russ flicked a glance toward the stairs.

"Don't move," I warned him, bringing the sword up another inch. He went very still. "You said my guardian angel looked away at a crucial moment and regretted it."

"Yes," Russ said quietly. "I *did* look away—and that's when *he* slipped in like a sneak-thief. One moment was all it took. I've been fighting to oust him from your life ever since, but it's not that easy. You loved him so much, it gave him a particularly strong hold over you. He's fallen, Suzanne—you know what that means? He has no Grace. He's a rebel. You call them demons, and they attach themselves to people and suck them dry of every joy your Creator gives you."

Raum's eyes stayed steady on my face. "He talks a pretty speech. I can say no more to convince you I'm being truthful. You'd best pray for guidance, because you're going to have to kill one of us. Your survival counts on you picking the right one."

"Don't listen to him," Russ pleaded. "See how even now he talks of killing? He'd make you a murderer if he could. That's how his kind separate you from grace. Put the sword down, Suzanne. You don't have to be a part of this. You don't have to murder."

I looked from Russ's pleading, earnest face to Raum's, expressionless and waiting. I lowered the sword an inch. Then two. And finally let it dangle from my hand, pointed toward the floor.

The hammering on the door was now accompanied by heavy thuds. A small battering ram. I'd seen one on COPS. I glanced toward the stairs, and instantly caught a movement from the corner of my eye, an aggressive action taking advantage of my momentary distraction.

A bolt of pure sensation shot through me, bringing alive every molecule of my being. I whirled around and raised the sword, not feeling my broken arm or my blistered feet or the cuts on my hands and feet from the broken glass. I felt strong, invincible, superhuman, as I swung the blade in a smooth arc toward the fallen angel who rushed me, teeth bared for the killing blow.

Chapter Eight

Shattered.

The world exploded, blinding light like a billion prisms in the sun, and then pain roared through my body, so excruciating I was certain I could not survive it.

Fractured.

I came to consciousness in fragments, every nerve ending in my body screaming in agony.

Splintered.

Pieces of me lay scattered like shining splinters of crystal. I gathered them frantically, scooping up great heaps of razor-edged shards of Suzanne, patting them into place with bloodied hands.

But parts were missing. Nothing fit right. Essential portions of me had been crushed into fine, shimmering flakes and set to drift on otherworldly winds.

"Suzanne."

No, no time to talk. I had to put me back together, splinter by splinter, like a jigsaw puzzle from hell. One sliver at a time, each drawing blood, until the floor ran slick with it, a river of red carrying away important chunks. I snatched at them, sobbing desperately, only to lose others to the flood.

"Suzanne." The voice prodded me, insistent this time. I turned, and the river of blood carried way yet more of me. "Wake up."

I opened my eyes to stare into eternity. Flares of color drifted through the gem-like depths. And then it moved away, resolving into two orbs like windows into heaven.

Eyes. Angel eyes.

"Can you understand me? We have little time." An arm beneath my shoulders lifted me from the floor. I struggled in protest, not wanting to slosh through the blood. He persisted, gently haranguing me until I sat upright, gasping and shaking.

There was no river carrying away splinters of me. There *was* blood, both Ian's and mine, and shards of broken glass and shattered drywall. But I still felt like parts of me were missing, and now, staring up at him, I knew what parts those were. The bindings that had tied me to the *malakhim* were broken.

"Oh God, I—" I choked on the words. "I killed him!" The world spun and it was only with great effort that I managed not to throw up.

"Yes." He crouched before me, staring at me intently. "How did you know which one of us to kill?"

I shook my head. The details were still so muzzy. "I don't . . . it was just . . . " I tried to think, pushing aside the persistent memory of my splintered, bloody dream. "He worked too hard to convince me you were the killer. And there's the fine line between killing and murder, a line he wanted to pretend wasn't there."

"I'd have thought him taking you to a cemetery rather than a church for the shielding would have clued you in. Did I teach you nothing, Suzanne?"

I shrugged weakly.

"And then his taking you through our realm on a six-week starvation trek should have been enough to convince you of his guilt." Raum grinned a little, folding his legs under him to sit yoga-style in front of me.

I smiled, surprised that I could do so and relieved that it felt good. "There's that, too." My smile faded. "Why did he choose me?"

His grin faded too. "He's been after you for quite some time. In fact, the night you saw me on the roof—the night we met—he was poking around, trying to find a way around our defenses."

"*Our* defenses?" I repeated.

"With a demon like Icarus after you, you don't think I was the only one protecting you, do you? I'm just the only one you saw, because I wasn't being careful enough."

I frowned at the thought of being completely oblivious to a stalking demon—and to my heavenly guard. "It's because of what I did to Zanna, isn't it? That's why he noticed me."

His smile was kind. "Like you're the first one to make a mistake, Suzanne. He probably would only have tormented you a little, prodded you farther into immoral behavior, but for me."

"Mortal enemies?"

"*Immortal* enemies," he corrected. "We'd been friends. I was there when Michael cast them from heaven. I chose not to rebel, and he's been needling me ever since. When he realized I was your guardian, it increased his desire to get to you."

I digested this silently. To think of another realm of unseen beings able to interact so closely with mine, able to persuade and lead us astray without our ever suspecting their influence, was disconcerting.

"It is not your fault that Zanna is dead," he said quietly. "It's mine."

"Wasn't anyone protecting her?" I couldn't help my accusatory tone.

"We tried," Raum said sadly. "But she was so deep in her bitterness, and making very bad choices, that there were more of *them* around her than there were of us."

"But he already had you—why did he wait so long to get me? You were out of the way."

"You had other protectors, so you had to go with him willingly. Once he shielded you, no one could find you. He had to lay the trail—the other murders—and he had to lay it carefully so you would believe I was the killer. He's a patient fellow, but he's also somewhat stupid. It never occurred to him that you would have regrets about stealing Ian from Zanna; it meant he had to work a little harder. And remember—three years is barely any time for us. He probably had to scramble to get everything in place in that short a time."

I thought I understood now. "So he weakened me by the long journey, dumped me off on Ian, and then lured me up to the attic where he tried to convince me to kill you for him."

"Precisely. That would have changed things dramatically. With the strongest of your protectors out of the way, with you having murdered an innocent being, you would have been easy pickings."

"He would have killed me slowly, you mean."

Raum shook his head, his mouth tightening. "He almost certainly would have killed Ian right away—or made you do it. I don't think he would have killed you for many years. But it would have pleased him to drive you farther and farther away from forgiveness and redemption after how hard we worked to protect you from him."

Strangely enough, that made perfect sense to me. But Russ was dead now, and my need for protection not as pressing. "What now, Raum?"

He looked down at his hands, clasped together and dangling in the space between his folded legs. "Now I put things right. Well," he amended. "I can never put things right, really—too many people have died. But I can put things as right as I can— for you and Ian, anyway."

I stared at him, remembering something Russ had said. *When it's all settled and he's dealt with, I can take away the memory of all of this.*

"You mean you'll make it all go away. You'll take away the memory of . . . of everything."

"Not quite. I can't completely take away the memories—too much has happened outside of our little trio here. Zanna, for instance." His eyes flicked to Ian, who lay in an unconscious sprawl beside me. "There are scars, both physical and

76

emotional, that can't be totally erased."

My hand drifted up to right breast, where his mark still scarred my flesh. "It won't go away?"

"His bond canceled mine as soon as you accepted it, and you broke his bond when you killed him. You're free of us," he said gently. "The physical scars will never go away, but your memory of how you got them will change."

"Maybe I don't want it to. Maybe I'd rather live with the memories."

"It doesn't work that way. Love has to be strictly human for you, Suzanne. Those are the rules."

"And love for you has to be—?"

"Strictly divine." His smile was somewhat sad, but behind the sorrow was a transcendent joy I knew could never be matched with a human relationship. "Are you ready?"

"Wait," I said quickly, wanting to hold onto him for just a few minutes longer. "I know I won't remember any of this, but I want to know—where did Russ's body go?"

"No body," he replied promptly. "We're nothing but energy, forced into a shape." I arched a brow. "That's all you are too, you know, just energy, but in a different way than us."

"So all those times we . . . er . . . "

His smile blossomed. "Electrifying, yes?" I couldn't help but laugh. "Now is the time to say goodbye, Suzanne. The police will want through that door—" He motioned to the attic stairs "—and I'm expected to resume my duties as your guardian. And nothing more." He frowned sternly, as though I had suggested something indecent.

I could do this. Hadn't I proven I was brave? I'd just spent the last six weeks in the presence of a lethal fallen angel, after all, and struck him down when he would have killed me. But it was truly a slice of heaven being with Raum after so long, to drink in his face, to fall into those eyes that were so like verdant green meadows.

My voice quivered and tears spilled from my eyes as I said, "All right, then. Goodbye, Raum."

"Ah, Suzanne," he murmured and leaned forward, rocking up on his knees to press one last kiss on my lips.

Pain and light everywhere around me. Voices shouting, fingers prodding, hands lifting. Suffocating. I was suffocating. Gasping. Swirling blackness with tiny sparks of light. Then . . . nothing.

My hand flailed and clawed at the plastic oxygen mask. Cool fingers firmly grasped it and brought it to my side, strapping it down. Voices sang out numbers, words, that I couldn't comprehend in any sensible manner. An annoying wail rose above it all, shrieking and waning and shrieking and waning and...

I gave up trying to figure it all out, and let go of consciousness again.

When I next opened my eyes, it was to pale green walls and an IV drip in my good arm; the other was heavy with a plaster cast. A nurse in Marvin Martian scrubs bustled around my bed, changing the bag of fluid and taking vitals. She smiled when I opened my eyes.

"Well, look who's awake," she said soothingly. "Do you know where you are?"

"Hospital?" I posed it more as a question than an answer.

"Indeed. You've been through a lot, dear, so you just rest and don't worry about a thing."

You've been through a lot.

"What . . . happened to me?"

She goggled at me, and then realization dawned. "But you've been unconscious for a couple of days—head injury. Of course you wouldn't remember."

More than happy to fill in the blanks, she told me of my ordeal: kidnapped off the street by a serial killer, held in some unknown location for six weeks, starved and dehydrated, until I somehow escaped and walked in a complete daze to Ian's house—unaware that my captor had followed me. He got the jump on both Ian and me, and after an altercation in the attic, where he'd taken us—undoubtedly with the intent of murdering us—the police had shown up. Our attacker fled the scene, and Ian and I had been transported to the hospital with numerous injuries.

Well, that was my nutshell version; her version actually took much longer to tell, and not a lot of it made sense. Some of those gaps were filled in later when the police came to take my statement—such as they'd shown up at the penultimate moment because they were coming to ask me some follow-up questions from their interview two days before the last attack, an interview I didn't remember at all.

Since I'd sustained a concussion during the attack, the nurse assured me, it wasn't uncommon to lose the memories of several days or even weeks before the event after a head injury. I tried not to worry about it, but something felt wrong about the whole story. The pieces didn't fit quite right, but I had nothing else to fit in their place, so I accepted what I was told and tried to move on.

Ian was less complacent about the whole thing. He was released from the hospital the day after we were admitted, and after making sure I was going to be fine, he took a leave of absence from work and retreated to the depths of his Queen Anne, disconnecting both the phone and the doorbell. I suppose I couldn't blame him; there he'd been, minding his own business for the last five years since our break-up, and I show up on his doorstep out of the blue after having been missing for over a month, trailing mayhem and misery in my wake.

Not exactly the best way to get back into a man's good graces.

He asked me one question before leaving that even now, a year later, I still hadn't figured out how to answer.

"Why did you come to me, Suzanne? When you escaped, you could have gone to the police. You could have gone anywhere. So why did you come to me?"

In other words, why did you bring this crap to *my* doorstep?

I stared out across the park toward Puget Sound, frowning a little. The police had asked me the same question, and the only answer I could give was I hadn't been thinking clearly in my traumatized state.

The real answer was "No idea." And the question no one had thought to ask but which haunted me day and night was: how had I found Ian's house? I'd had no clue where he lived, and yet I walked there when I escaped.

Some questions had no answers. I would have to be content never knowing precisely what happened to me, and find a way to live with the gaping holes and the disquiet they caused.

The bank welcomed me back with relief. An extra security guard was hired for the main purpose of making sure my assailant never had another chance to nab me. The fact that he'd never been caught worried them greatly, but me—well, something deep inside me said I'd seen the last of him.

I still felt that essential pieces of me—of the me I'd known before all this happened—were missing, but maybe they weren't bad pieces. One day a subordinate remarked, "You seem different, Suzanne. Stronger, more at peace." She studied my face for a long, uncomfortable moment and then added, "And not as sad as you used to be."

Perhaps, but I couldn't explain why—because I didn't know. I rather suspected the reason lay within those missing pieces.

I turned away from the Sound to resume my jog, and for a second I saw from the corner of my eye what looked like a man made from a pillar of light. My heart leapt. It was—it was—

But I had no way to finish the thought. A second later, the man moved off to the east and I realized the sinking sun behind him had set him ablaze and made him appear to be made of light.

Laughing a little, I turned and began jogging back up the trail toward the parking lot. A small child, squealing with laughter, darted in front of me, followed by an older sibling, and I swerved around them to avoid a collision. My foot plunged into a hole more than likely dug by those same kids, and I crashed to earth, taking with me another jogger whose path had intersected mine at an inopportune moment.

"Oh, God," I said, rolling onto my rear. "I'm so sor—"

He raised his head, saw me and groaned, and flopped back onto the ground. "You'll be the death of me someday, Suze."

"I'm really sorry, Ian. I tried to avoid the kids and fell in a hole I'm sure they dug with the sole purpose of killing me."

His chuckle became a rolling laugh, and soon he was fairly howling. I smiled, a little puzzled, but by the time he'd gained control of himself, I was giggling a little myself.

Ian pushed himself to his feet, looked at me for a long moment, squinting against the sun, and then reached down to haul me upright. He brushed the dirt and grass from his clothes and his bare legs.

"Come on," he said, grinning with a hint of his old charm. "Let's go get a drink."

He started off toward the parking lot, and I fell into step beside him. Halfway there, his hand swung back and bumped against mine. Our fingers twined.

A peculiar feeling of déjà vu crept over me, the first of many, but I pushed it aside. Too much trouble to chase it down, and it would lead to a dead end anyway. I let it go.

And finally, I knew peace.

THE STONE GARDEN

A Devil's Mansion Short Story
by Sharon Gerlach

Sunday

The elegant manor weathered the centuries with a stoic, stately grace. Though many hands had applied their own style, the interior remained true to its original Gothic Revival design. Families came and went, and between their occupation the house remained vacant, the dust of the ages collecting in the corners and passageways. No one stayed long, for misfortune seemed the lot of any who owned the mansion.

The sweeping grounds included a formal garden, and here it was that Mia Talbot, the new mistress of Blessing House, found the stone garden. Not *made* of stone, you see, for the beds were lush and immaculate even when the house was unoccupied. No one saw the discreet caretakers who came; they were paid well to be unobtrusive and closed-mouthed regarding the many strange happenings on the grounds. The stone garden was so called for the lifelike statues dotting a section of the landscaped grounds.

"Who is the artist?" Mia inquired of her husband. Her hand lay lightly upon his arm, which was bent at the crook to accommodate her. Sensible black pumps crunched the gravel under her feet as they traveled a safe and cautious path amongst the statuary.

"No one knows," replied her husband. Harold Talbot—Hal for short—straightened his tie and sent a glare into the gardens, as though warning the dirt to not even attempt to molest his smart business suit. A financial executive in New

York City, this move to a country estate outside Stamford, Connecticut proved no small amount of trouble for him. But with the death of their small daughter Abigail, Mia had lapsed into a deep depression and the Blessing House seemed peaceful and soothing.

"They didn't just *appear*, Hal," she said now, laughing. Her tea-length dress swished about her calves in a flirtatious manner, and she tugged on the thick woolen shawl shrouding her shoulders. Fog pressed in on the grounds, lying thick in the dips and gullies, drifting as formless wraiths across higher ground. The autumnal chill was invigorating, bringing color to Mia's cheeks for the first time in months. The death of summer was heralded by the changing of the leaves; gold, scarlet, umber, and burnt orange, they fluttered past their feet in drifts of colorful decay, driven by gusts of wind rolling in from Stamford Harbor.

"That's just the point, Mia," Hal said patiently. "They *did* just appear. Each time the house has changed hands, new statues appear. The artist is unknown, and they say the statuary resembles the departed owners."

Mia chuckled. The wind whipped a glossy lock of her short, black hair into her eyes, and she brushed it away, tucking it behind her ear. Hal scanned his wife's face with concern, noting the pallor that made the sprinkling of freckles stand out on her cheekbones and the bridge of her nose. Pale and dark-haired with light grey eyes, Mia's beauty was envied throughout their social circle, but her gentle, kind ways made her an easy target for vicious, gossiping tongues. Yes, better for her to remain in seclusion for a time while she learned to cope with the loss of Abigail.

"Come," he said, grasping her elbow. "You should go inside before you catch ill. It would be—"

"Oh, look, Hal!" she exclaimed in delight. "Look at the children!"

And indeed the statuary had given way to a grouping of children, playing about in all stages of activity. Here, a group of boys, stone berets set at jaunty angles as they bent to their work: a serious game of marbles. The marbles themselves lay at the base of one such statue, by the knee of a particularly lovely lad. Girls played jump rope games, the swirl and swish of their school dresses fantastically captured by the sculptor, as were the very threads and cables of the rope itself. Mia laughed in delight to find a toddler with a marble frog poking from his pocket; a young girl with a handful of posies and a cricket in her hair; and a boy with his puppy trotting faithfully at his heel.

"Very clever," said Hal uneasily. And yes, the sculptures were exquisite, the details incredibly lifelike, but he found them rather sinister.

Mia slanted him a look from the corner of her eye, catching his expression of distaste and worry. "Oh, very well, mother hen. Let's go back to the house and have a hot cup of tea. You've a long drive back to New York tomorrow."

"It's not that long, Mia," he said, guiding her with relief out of the stone garden and back toward the mansion. "Only fifty miles."

"An hour each way," she pointed out. "Are there things you want me to do while you're away?"

Their talk turned to the more mundane issues at hand and the tasks he needed her to accomplish during his absence—all designed, she was sure, simply to keep her busy. Hal opened one of the French-paned doors to let her inside, and as he stepped through and closed it behind him, it seemed the house had swallowed them both.

Monday

Mia rattled around Blessing House after her list of tasks had been completed; Hal had not left her much to do during his week-long business conference in New York. A drizzling rain had kept her indoors, thwarting her plans to more fully investigate the stone garden. She'd dreamt of the statues instead, fantastical dreams that had been thrilling but now in the light of day seemed ominous.

She curled up on a sofa that faced the windows looking over the grounds. She could see the tops of the tallest sculptures, the rain gleaming like jewels on marble tresses. She longed to walk the paths and discover the chiseled delights farther into the garden. Really, Hal was so *cautious*; it wasn't as though she were so fragile she would break in two if she exerted herself. He worried incessantly since her emotional collapse, but that had been immediately following the accident. She still dreamed of it: the February chill that left a layer of black ice on the road, the uncontrollable skid that sent the car careening down the embankment beside the bridge instead of across it, the seatbelt catch that wouldn't release until Abigail had already drowned.

Fog rolled in from the harbor, wrapping the statuary in gauzy layers of white. Mia's head dropped to the back of the sofa, and she slept.

"Mommy, Mommy! Catch me if you can!" Dark curls dancing in the damp air, Abigail ran ahead of her into the stone garden, a miniature Mia in an organdy dress and blue woolen coat.

"Abby, wait!" One part of her was surprised to see her daughter, for Abigail had never been to Blessing House. Another part seemed to make sense of the young girl's presence, and this part led her laughing after Abby.

"Come, Mommy! Come deeper into the garden! There's something I want to show you!"

And so Mia picked up her step, trotting after her daughter as fast as her pumps and dress would allow. Abby waited on the path ahead of her, and just when Mia thought she would catch the little scamp, Abigail darted ahead again, giggling.

Deeper and deeper into the garden, until the light began to fade from the day and ephemeral curtains of fog prevented her from seeing more than two feet before her. Mia paused, unable to see Abby although she could hear her.

"Abby! It's time to go back to the house now. It's getting dark and foggy; I can't see you!"

Childish giggles echoed through the fog. It was impossible to tell where Abigail had gone although Mia thought she was close by.

"Abby!" Fear threaded her voice. Oh, to lose her in the garden in the fog—Hal would be livid!

But what was she thinking? Abigail had died in the car accident; she could not be here at Blessing House.

"Come play, Mia!" a child's sibilant whisper coaxed her. "We want to play. Will you stay and play with us?"

Mia whirled around. Had the sound come from behind her? Or from the left? Impossible to tell. "Who are you?"

"We live in the garden, Mia. Will you stay with us? We want you to stay!"

"Mommy, please stay! Don't you want to stay with me?"

But now Abigail's voice seemed sinister, her tone threatening. Fear washed over Mia and she fled to the house, the laughter of the children seeming to mock her as she ran.

Tuesday

Dearest Hal,

Today was a lovely clear day. I walked through the stone garden and finally saw all the statuary. Don't worry, I didn't overdo it. There are wonderful little benches all along the paths, and I rested often on these and studied the statues. They really *are* remarkable, Hal. So lifelike you can almost hear them at play. My favorite so far is a grouping of three small girls sitting on a blanket with a litter of kittens crawling on them. It reminded me of Abigail, but I didn't cry. Truly, Hal, I didn't.

I miss you terribly and look forward to your return.

Yours,
Mia

Wednesday

Mia stared at her reflection with dismay. Oh, her skin! So dry and itchy from the ocean air. It felt rough to the touch but not flaky, almost like rough stone waiting to be polished. She slathered her body with expensive moisturizing cream, her fingers stiff and reluctant. Her limbs were heavy and awkward today, and after an uncomfortable two hours on the sofa, staring into the gardens, she went back up to her bed.

She dreamed she played with the kittens, and the girls giggled and piled on top of her, and for the first time in months Mia was happy.

Thursday

Dearest Hal,

I didn't rise today until after noon. All night I had strange dreams about the statues of the children. They wanted me to come out and play, and at first I was frightened, but...one of them reminded me of Abby, so I went. We played ring-around-the-rosy and duck-duck-goose and sang songs. And then I woke...oh, Hal, I miss Abigail so much!

This sea air is invigorating and I enjoy it, but it is drying my skin terribly. I feel lethargic and stiff all over and am comfortable only when I lay still and quiet on the bed. I'm sure it will pass. Perhaps when you return, we can go into the city and pick up some of the cream that works so well. It would be nice to have a late dinner in the city and perhaps stay the night in a posh hotel. I often feel isolated here even with the servants to converse with.

Come home soon, darling!

Your loving wife,

Mia

Friday

Cold, so cold! Mia huddled under the blankets, shivering, each tremor sending shooting pain through her limbs. The roughness of her skin was fading in patches, leaving behind flesh as smooth as polished marble. But her fingers skated over those patches as though over ice and she did not feel them, not their warmth or their caress.

Mia pulled the thick wool blanket from the foot of the bed over her quaking body, crying with every agonizing move. Finally she laid back, the shivers subsiding, and she was still and quiet.

Fog puddled on the ground, shrouding her feet as she confidently walked the paths of the stone garden. Although the October day was cold, she wore no jacket. She didn't need one.

The gravel crunched beneath her feet and the girls looked up as she approached. Smiles wreathed their faces, and Mia thought they seemed more human and less statue than they had before. The kittens scampered to her, clustering around her feet. She could nearly see color in their fur now: calico, grey tiger-striped, Russian blue.

"Are you staying with us, Mia? Please stay!"

"Please, Mia! We're all alone!"

"Don't go this time! Stay and play with us!"

Mia considered. "Yes, I'll stay."

The children cheered and the kittens wound about her ankles, meowing frantically. Mia stooped to pick up the calico and found the ache and chill had left her limbs. The day was glorious and bright, the sun setting fire to the crimson leaves lying in drifts at the edge of the grounds. Girls with golden curls and black tresses and red ringlets crowded round her, their pretty plaid skirts swishing about their knee-high socks, their patent leather shoes scuffed from play.

Mia laughed joyfully. "Oh yes, I'll stay!

Saturday

The police had finally left after sweeping the grounds and asking a passel of uncomfortable questions. Hal Talbot didn't mind.; if it would help them find Mia, he would face disconcerting inquisitions for the rest of eternity.

He'd returned home to find Mia missing and the servants bewildered. A packet of letters lay on his pillow as always; Mia usually wrote him every day when he travelled, and left them for him to read when he returned home if his trip was short. The letters concerned him; she had obviously fallen ill and he worried that she had become delirious and wandered the countryside.

Moonlight gleamed on the heads of the tallest statues, and Hal shrugged into his coat and pushed through the French doors and into the stone garden. His steps took him on a wandering journey through the statuary, deep into the grounds. In the glow from the hunter's moon, the white marble masterpieces glowed like spirits brought to earth to play amongst the lavender and late-flowering chrysanthemum. Hal found himself enchanted and although he tried, he couldn't quite shake it off.

The path brought him to a bed where an arrangement of chiseled little girls and kittens frolicked under the watchful eye of a beautiful woman. She held a tiny kitten to her cheek and smiled softly at the girls at play. Hal thought she resembled Mia to a remarkable degree.

The whisper floated softly to him on the night wind:

"Hal, come and play with us! Will you stay? We want you to stay!"

Alarmed, he turned in a circle. "Who's there?"

"Please, Hal, say you'll come with us. We want you to come!" Mia's voice, seducing him, enticing him.

Hal laid a hand against the cold marble cheek of his

wife's likeness and answered as though in a
dream, "Yes, I'll come."

THE WYCKHAM HOUSE
The Devil's Mansion Book One

By Sharon Gerlach

October 28, 2004—10:00 a.m.

How do I get myself into these situations?

The shadowy ceiling offered no answers, not that Kimberly could have read them anyway in the flickering light of the torch. But of course she didn't need the ceiling to point out a few home truths. She was in this situation through her own foolhardiness: a stolen identity, swiped from her best friend, to whom she bore a striking resemblance; a reckless, half-assed plan to find her father, whom she wasn't even sure was missing; and falling in love with the wrong man.

She shifted on the unyielding stone surface, and the links of her chains clinked like chimes. She was caught as surely as a rabbit in a snare; chewing her arm off seemed a drastic step to free herself, although if her bladder wasn't given relief soon it would seem like a fine idea.

He would come for her, of course; nothing would stop him. She wished he wouldn't. He would be given no reprieve this time; they would finish the job they had started years ago, silencing him forever. And what of her? There were worse things than death; he had been right about that.

It was her fault her father was missing as well. Had she begged off gathering his requested research—after all, she had deadlines of her own and little time to spare—perhaps he wouldn't have had the information that led him to his suspicions about this town.

But that was only supposition and a bit of her habit of taking the blame for things that weren't her responsibility.

Todd must have already suspected what lay behind the strange animal attacks and unexplained disappearances, or he would not have asked for the particular information she'd collected.

Finally, she had to acknowledge the fact that she'd been warned away. The danger was real, the potential for mortal disaster unequivocal. And yet here she was, strapped to an ancient stone altar in the bowels of the house of the devil himself, lying in a pool of blood still tacky to the touch. The blood of a friend.

Quiet footsteps brought her head around; her hair stuck to the altar, and she fought a wave of nausea as she pulled it free. She'd grown used to the scent of blood over the last two hours, but when she moved, it wafted strong and cloying on the air and coated her tongue with bitter copper, like licking the end of a battery. Her stomach rolled.

He appeared out of the gloom like a violent apparition: her captor, the man who held her fate in his bloodstained, murderous hands. He moved with a fluid grace common to his family, as though he were liquid contained in a human shape. The darkness didn't seem to bother him, and not for the first time she wondered what gifts he'd been given in exchange for his soul.

"How are we doing?" His soulless eyes held a glint of mocking laughter.

"I don't know about you, but I could really use the restroom."

"Just came from there myself, but thank you for your concern." He extended no offer of relief to her, not that she had expected him to. He seemed determined to drive her to such a point of discomfort that she would release her bladder to mingle with the blood on the stone. But damned if she was going to add that humiliation to her already dismal circumstances.

Which brought her to another of her failings: she should have been more cautious, more suspicious of everyone. She'd been bagged easily—too easily, almost as if by complicity she'd been placed exactly where he could catch her.

She turned away, her eyes going back to the dark shadows hovering above her, silently communicating her refusal to beg. He chuckled.

"It's simple, Kimberly. You know what I want: a simple bit of truthful information. Then I'll let you go."

Her head came back around. "You won't. You'll keep me captive until it suits you to either kill me or...worse. And I'm sure being in your captivity won't be pleasant. I've already experienced enough to know that much."

Involuntarily, her hand came up and massaged her bruised throat, leaving sticky prints of blood behind. At his widening smile, she damned herself for showing weakness. Yet another of her failings.

He leaned close. He smelled heavenly, like the woods after a heavy rain. How ironic that such an evil man could smell so divine. She tried not to breathe in; his scent clouded her mind with a hellish desire to fling herself at him and satisfy her carnal urges. It would be exquisite, she knew. Exquisite and satiating and shameful and damning. He would be cruel in his passion and passionate in his cruelty, and worse, he would own her then, body and surrendered soul.

His lips brushed her cheek as he spoke. She couldn't stop her shudder, and she told herself it was simple revulsion. But her pulse sped to a wild beat, and her body flared with sudden heat.

"Why did you say it? Who told you to say it? How did you know what she said before she died?"

"I don't know."

It was not the first time he'd asked, nor the first time she had no answer; she hadn't been aware of speaking at all. Her only memory of their altercation was of him catching her by her hair as she bolted for the back door and being pinned to the floor, his elegant fingers around her throat.

She was certain she had died, but perhaps that had been a dream while she had been unconscious. Otherwise, she would have to accept the fact that she had been brought back to life by the breath of an angel—a *real* angel—and that meant she would also have to accept that the driving force behind this man, behind his circle of black magic, was hell itself.

He offered no comment; her answer had been expected. His finger traced an indecent line down her cheek and over her throat, jumping the inadequate barricade of her collarbone, coming to rest in the valley between her breasts and hovering just above the first fastened button of her shirt. Add another of her failings: never dressing appropriately for the occasion.

Her heart galloped like a bolting horse, and his smile grew predatory. His eyes held her paralyzed; she'd never encountered someone who could hold one's gaze so unflinchingly for such a long time. She felt exposed, x-rayed, stripped down and distilled to her core by those cold eyes. She recognized the silent proposition in them and sent back her equally silent answer: *No. Not just no, but HELL no.*

"You might not appreciate the destination, but you will surely enjoy the journey."

"Physical satisfaction isn't everything."

His grin was thoroughly unholy, but he moved away from her, taking with him the tantalizing woodsy scent and his inhibition-erasing sensuality.

"You're taking this rather well, much better than most do. No weeping or begging. Very noble of you to accept your fate so philosophically and matter-of-factly."

"Will fighting you make any difference?"

"None." He leaned in again swiftly, startling her. She pressed back into the stone and instantly regretted it as copper scented the air. "Don't make me kill you, Kimberly," he whispered urgently. "Tell me what I want to know, and I'll let you live."

"As your captive."

"Yes."

"As your consort?" She lifted a brow.

"That goes without saying."

She turned her face away again, forcing her expression to lapse into careful indifference. "I'd rather die."

His rage could not be contained behind his impassive reaction. While he simply straightened from her and squared his shoulders, the very air around them vibrated with his fury. He pressed a finger painfully against her lips and took a step away from the altar.

"So be it."

AVAILABLE IN PRINT AND EBOOK FORMATS
AT MOST ONLINE RETAILERS

ABOUT THE AUTHOR

Sharon Gerlach was in training to be a ninja, but a dismaying lack of physical grace and balance--not to mention the inability to keep her big mouth shut--ended her ninja career before it had really begun. Now she writes. She doesn't write about ninjas because that's obviously a sore subject. But she writes about other really cool things and figures someone else will cover the ninjas. Life's really not all about ninjas, anyway.

Sharon lives on the dry side of the Pacific Northwest with her husband (who must really be fond of her as he hasn't left her yet despite her ninja failings); her three kids and a grandchild (none of whom possess ninja qualities either); and a Border collie who suffers the presence of six cats. Yes, you guessed it--ninja cats!

Website: sharongerlach.com
Twitter: @SharonGerlach
Facebook Page: AuthorSharonGerlach

www.ingramcontent.com/pod-product-compliance
Lightning Source LLC
Chambersburg PA
CBHW020622130626
46552CB00003B/1076